Intersections at Mayfield and Green
Stories of South Euclid's First Century

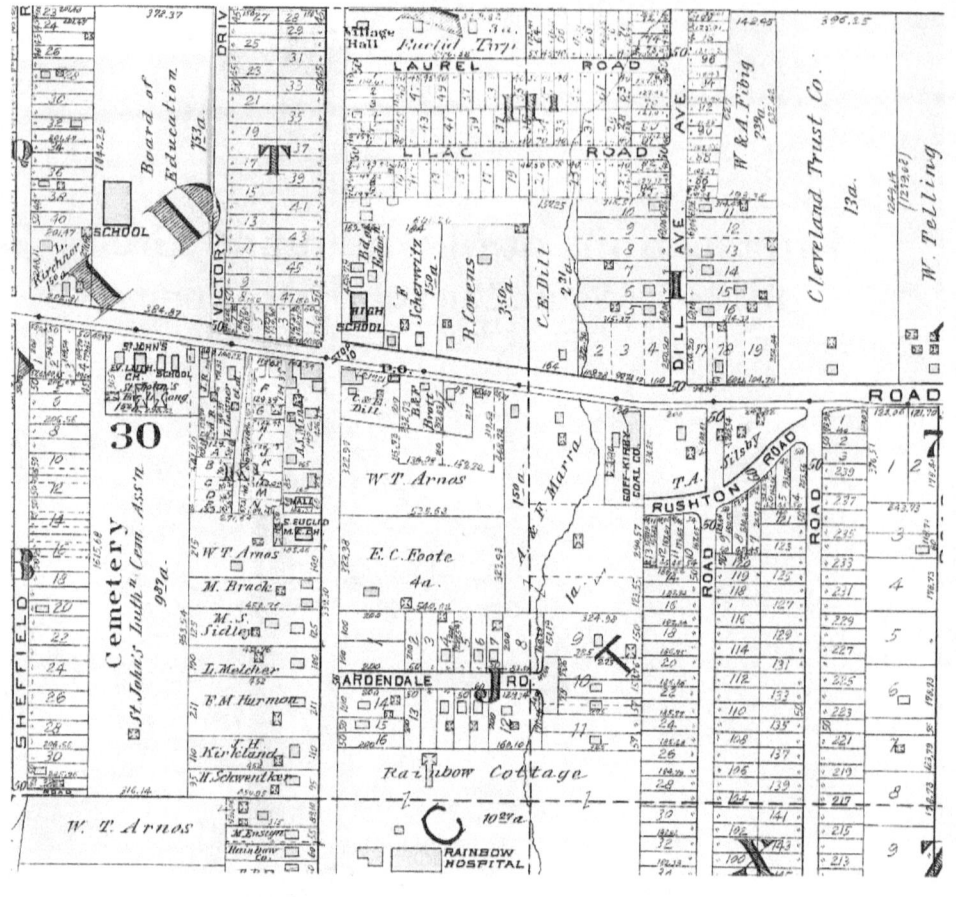

Hopkins 1920 Plat Map Vol. 3 of Cuyahoga County,
Plate 16 showing the Intersections and More [CPLDL]

Intersections at Mayfield and Green
Stories of South Euclid's First Century

Written by Students at Notre Dame College

Foreword by Hon. Georgine Welo
Mayor of South Euclid

Illustrations by Megan Dull SND MFA

Edited by Eileen Quinlan SND PhD

South Euclid-Lyndhurst Historical Society Publications
2017

First Printing: 2017

ISBN 978-0-692-84796-1

Library of Congress No.: 2017904245

South Euclid – Lyndhurst Historical Society Publications
4629 Mayfield Road
South Euclid, OH 44121

SE-Lhistory.org

Ordering Information:

Special discounts are available on quantity purchases by corporations, associations, educators, and others. For details, contact the publisher at the above listed address.

U.S. trade bookstores and wholesalers: Please contact South Euclid – Lyndhurst Historical Society Publications Tel: (216) 970-2333; or email Info@SE-Lhistory.org

Dedication

To the young people of South Euclid,

who will shape the community's next century.

Contents

Acknowledgements

Beginning in the spring semester of 2012 and continuing through the fall of 2016, eighteen Notre Dame College students committed their time, creativity, talent, patience and enthusiasm to the work of researching, writing, revising and editing these stories. I am grateful to the students in Ohio Writers, American Literature, and Local Fiction Writing who wrote five of these stories as class assignments, and to the students who wrote two stories for the simple joy they found in research and writing.

These stories would not have their accuracy of detail without the gracious cooperation of these individuals who provided information, pictures, stories, tours, time and enthusiasm for the project: Dr. Roy Berko; Margaret Burzynski-Bays, University Hospitals Archives; Mr. Larry Cirillo; Ms. Patricia Harding, Archivist of Notre Dame College; Ms. Carol Holliger, Archives of Ohio United Methodism; Mr. Dominick Kaple, Principal of Memorial Junior High School; Rabbi Roger C. Klein; Mr. Bob McKimm, South Euclid-Lyndhurst Historical Society; Ms. Lindsay Miller, Maltz Museum of Jewish Heritage; Chief Kevin Nietert, South Euclid Police Department; Sr. Renee Pastor and the Class of 2017 of St. Francis School, Cleveland; Ms. Karen Poelking, Notre Dame College Vice President for Board and Community Relations; Mr. Carter Welo, South Euclid True Value Hardware; Ms. Wendy Wasman, Cleveland Museum of Natural History; Mr. John Williams, Euclid Historical Museum; Sr. Elizabeth Wood, Archivist of the Sisters of Notre Dame, Chardon; Karen Zoller, Director of the Clara Fritzsche Library; my Notre Dame College colleagues Jacqi Loewy, Anita Pajek, Roslyn Scheer-McLeod, and Dalma Takacs; and Regina High School graduates Laurie Divoky SND, Carol McHenry SND, Beverly Walter Schweickert, Carole Prochaska Smith, Pamela Wright Waitinas, and Joanne Zeitz SND.

The writers and I also extend gratitude for the professionalism and kindness of staff members at the Cuyahoga County Archives, Garfield Memorial Church (formerly South Euclid-Hillcrest United Methodist Church), Sacred Heart of Jesus Parish (formerly St. Gregory the Great Parish), the South Euclid-Lyndhurst Board of Education, and the Western Reserve Historical Society.

ILLUSTRATIONS

The pinwheel logo of South Euclid's Centennial is used by permission, line drawings by Megan Dull SND MFA; map courtesy of Cleveland Public Library's Digital Library; photos page 12, Bluestone Quarry, South Euclid – Lyndhurst Historical Society [SE-LHS]; 14, Bluestone Mills [SE-LHS]; 24, League Park, Western Reserve Historical Society [WR]; 25, Napoleon Lajoie, Unknown [UNK]; 30, Interurban Railroad Car [SE-LHS]; 32, League Park, Cleveland Memories [CM]; 37, Green Road School [SE-LHS]; 39 St. Gregory Church [SE-LHS]; 40, Nowak Villa, Stanley A. Ferguson Archives, University Hospitals [UH], 51, Hudson's Gas Station [SE-LHS]; 52, Brush High School [SE-LHS]; 61, South Euclid City Hall [SE-LHS]; 71, War Memorial Dedication [SE-LHS]; 78, Regina High School, Notre Dame College Archives [NDC]; 79 NDC Administration Building [NDC]; 83, Chemistry Lab, [NDC]; 89, Memorial Jr. High [UNK]

Eileen Quinlan SND PhD
Professor of English
Notre Dame College
Editor

Foreword

I moved to South Euclid, Ohio, in 1979 as a young bride because it was my husband Carter's hometown. For Carter, South Euclid was an active and vital place with great people and a diversity of neighborhoods. South Euclid was (and always will be) home to him and where he wanted to live, raise a family and own a business. Once I settled in, I realized why he liked his hometown so much. As the years passed and I became more active in the community, I had the great pleasure to meet many generations of South Euclid residents and experience our community's unique history through their stories, many passed down through several generations. Many of these residents were like Carter: they grew up in South Euclid with their parents and remained in the community to raise their own families.

In a very short time, I realized how special a place South Euclid was, and it wasn't long before it became "home" to me and I could recite all of the historic places and things that built our great community. We have historic institutions like Notre Dame College (a private college opened in 1922 by the Sisters of Notre Dame that set down roots in South Euclid four years later) and Rainbow Hospital, founded in 1905 by a group called the Circle of King's Daughters to help and care for disabled children. And there are so many other local "family" stories like the settlements of the Western Reserve along old Indian trails, historic businesses like the Saw Mill, Prasse Basket Factory, Bluestone Quarry, Livery Stable and the family estates of the Palermos and William E. Telling along Mayfield Road.

In addition, our community's rich natural landscape runs from Cedar Road (named for the trees that lined it), to the interurban "Red Cars" along Mayfield Road, to the numerous creeks and streams that run quietly throughout the city to fill Euclid Creek as it heads towards our Great Lake Erie. There was the old Euclid Railroad which transported the cut stone north from the South Euclid quarries at South

Belvoir and Monticello Boulevards (now home to our Quarry Park) and hauled them down to Euclid Avenue, where they were used to build many of Cleveland's first sidewalks and streets.

South Euclid is about more than just its history. South Euclid was and continues to be a mixture of rural and urban, with easy connections to both Cleveland on the west and the more rural communities to the east. Today we remain a richly diverse, vital and vibrant community with many styles of homes, unique neighborhoods, revitalized business districts with a good mix of national and local retail, and a great system of parks and open greenspace.

Most importantly, South Euclid today is filled with active, caring and thoughtful people who care about the future of their community and work hard to make sure that it remains a safe, stable, vibrant and unique place to call home. In all of my nearly 30 years of public service, I am most thankful for the great residents that continue to support our city, schools, parks and businesses.

Just as my husband Carter shared his love for his hometown, I deeply cherish my 38 years here in South Euclid. This book, *Intersections at Mayfield and Green: Stories of South Euclid's First Century*, offers historical insights of the past along with creative fiction to help shape a picture of the first 100 years. This publication by Notre Dame College students also serves to promote open discussion on a variety of community-related topics and makes clear that history can be a powerful way of sharing what continues to make South Euclid a vital and vibrant place to live, work and play.

I hope residents of all ages will take the time to read and enjoy the stories in this powerful and insightful book, and on the occasion of South Euclid's 100th Anniversary, keep working to continue to keep South Euclid a great place to "Come Together and Thrive."

Georgine Welo, Mayor
South Euclid, Ohio
1 February 2017

Preface

A centennial is a grand observance for a community. It provides an opportunity for long-time residents and those who grew up in the community but have since moved away to share stories and revel in, or rue, the changes they've seen over the years. But a hundred years is an enormous span of time for a child, and adults' memories, vivid as they may be, can be ancient history for teenagers. The goal of this anthology is to give young people some windows into life in the South Euclid community during its earlier history. These stories take place in the vicinity of the intersection of Mayfield and Green, imagining the lives of young people at home and at school, at work and at play.

Since the early nineteenth century, at least, the intersection of Mayfield Road (once called the old State Road, and later the Mayfield Plank Road) and Green Road has been a crossroads for farmers and merchants, commuters and locals, and children. Generations of children have walked through this intersection on the way to and from school—to the Old Stone School and the Green Road School, to St. John's and St. Gregory's, to Victory Park and Regina, to the Lyceum and Memorial and Brush.

In these stories, the characters' lives intersect with the lives of people who are familiar to them, and with the lives of newcomers to the community. Through the years, the people of this community have learned how to "come together and thrive." It is our hope that today's schoolchildren and young people, like the young people in these stories, can continue to welcome strangers and invite them to become friends in the second century of the community that is South Euclid.

Introduction

While these stories and their main characters are purely fictional, the writers used their research to situate the stories in the actual life and times of Mayfield-Green and Greater Cleveland.

An Invitation and a Decision: A Story of South Euclid in 1883

In 1883, the fictional Liam Donovan works at the real McFarland Quarry, located in the present-day Euclid Creek Reservation of the Cleveland Metroparks. In 1883, architect Charles Schweinfurth began his Cleveland career with the construction of the Sylvester Everett mansion on Euclid Avenue near present-day East 40th Street, then called Case Avenue. The Methodist community in southern Euclid Township built their first church on Mayfield Road in 1883 while they were part of the charge of Rev. John H. Tagg of the Methodist Church in Nottingham village, still in South Collinwood at 18316 St. Clair Avenue.

It Was Worth It: A Story of South Euclid in 1915

During his years as the star second baseman for Cleveland's baseball team (1902-14), Napoleon Lajoie and his wife Myrtle owned property near the northwest corner of Mayfield and Richmond. Even after he went to the Philadelphia Athletics in 1915, the couple continued to call Greater Cleveland home. Known in 1914 as the Cleveland Naps (in honor of Lajoie), the Cleveland team played at League Park on Lexington Avenue. The Cleveland & Eastern streetcar line ran along Mayfield Road from 1895 until 1926, ferrying passengers and freight between downtown Cleveland and Gates Mills, Chardon and Middlefield. In 1912, the old stone schoolhouse on the northeast corner of Mayfield and Green was replaced by a two-story red brick building on the same site housing elementary and high school classes until Victory Park Elementary School (on the site of the present-day Giant Eagle store) opened in 1921, and Brush High School in 1927.

Finding the Courage: A Story of South Euclid in 1925

In the early years of the twentieth century, as immigrants to northern Ohio moved outward from the central city, the farming hamlet centered at Mayfield and Green rapidly became a diversified village with citizens of many nationalities, religions and occupations. St. Gregory the Great Parish was established by the Diocese of Cleveland in 1922, with Fr. Maurice A. Riley as pastor. Rainbow Hospital for Crippled and Convalescent Children began in Cleveland as Rainbow Cottage in 1896, and occupied several locations before re-opening in 1904 in the Novak Villa, a large frame house on Green Road where University Suburban Health Center now stands. In 1928 Rainbow Hospital was built on the site, specializing in treating children with orthopedic issues. The South Euclid-Lyndhurst School District staffed a classroom in the Rainbow building. Although Rainbow Hospital's services were moved to the main campus of University Hospitals in 1971, Rainbow Road is a reminder of the hospital's presence in the city.

The Heist and What Came of It: A Story of South Euclid in 1935

During the Great Depression, Hudson's Gas Station was a landmark on the northwest corner of Mayfield and Green. While several grocery stores served downtown South Euclid over the years, Mr. Schantz is a fictional character. In 1928 William Telling, owner of the Telling-Belle Vernon Company, commissioned the mansion at 4645 Mayfield Road, on the south edge of his dairy farm. The building served as a branch of the Cuyahoga County Library from 1951 to 2015. Douglas G. Oviatt was the mayor of South Euclid from 1932 to 1945, and Martin Schmies was Chief of Police from 1941-1961. Rev. Walter O. Bischoff was pastor at St. John Lutheran from 1922 until his death in 1949, just weeks before the dedication of the War Memorial.

Farewells and New Beginnings:
A Story of South Euclid in 1949

After World War II, Cleveland's Jewish community began a gradual migration from the Glenville and Mt. Pleasant neighborhoods to the Heights communities. Memorial Junior High School opened in February 1949, eventually serving seventh-, eighth- and ninth-graders. The city's War Memorial was dedicated on Sunday September 11, 1949, on the grounds of Victory Park School. In 1985 it was relocated to the intersection of Green and Anderson Roads.

Finding Her Own Way: A Story of South Euclid in 1956

Opened in 1953 on Green Road near Notre Dame College, Regina High School provided secondary education for girls until closing in 2011. The Sisters of Notre Dame named in the story were on staff at Regina in its early years. Geraci's Pizza opened in July of 1956 on the southwest corner of Cedar and Green before moving to Warrensville Center Road near Silsby in 1958.

Outsiders, Insiders, and a Few Simple Gifts:
A Story of South Euclid in 1975

The 1980 U.S. Census provides the first evidence of African-Americans living in South Euclid. The public schools integrated peacefully during the 1970s and 1980s. Mr. Larry Cirillo was an assistant principal at Memorial Junior High School in 1975; he served as a teacher and administrator there from 1956 to 1995. The other teachers in the story are fictional.

An Invitation and a Decision:
A Story of South Euclid in 1883

The high white clouds on this May morning were a world away from the noise in the quarry. The sledge hammers smashing against wedges and stone, the whir of the saws, the jangle of the teams' harnesses and the rattle of slatted wagons over the gravel, all the sound bounced off the rock face of the quarry on three sides. Liam knew the creek was pouring over the shale in a cool clear torrent, but the sound of it wouldn't reach his ears before dusk. So he was stunned to hear Mr. Manning's voice.

"Donovan! Donovan, get over here!" Mr. Manning had his straw hat pushed back, his hands on his hips, standing above the sawmill's sluiceway. Liam jumped off the wagon and sprinted down the incline toward the quarry owner, who stood talking with some fairly well-dressed men.

"Sir," Liam said, holding his cap, and stuffing his work gloves into his back pocket.

"Donovan, these gentlemen are interested in foundation stone. Would you show them the stock?" Manning nodded toward the shed of the finishing mill up toward the road.

"Surely, sir. This way, gentlemen." Liam led the way up the gravel road toward the sprawling wooden shed where enormous finished stone blocks were stacked near the rail line.

One of the younger men addressed the boy. "You're one of the youngest quarrymen I've seen on the lot. How old are you anyway? How long have you been with Manning?"

"I'm sixteen, sir. I've been here almost five years, I guess. I started here with my Da, and since he was hurt I've stayed on with the wagon crew. My name is Liam Donovan. My Da started here with old Mr. McFarland when we came from County Clare."

"Well, hello, Liam Donovan from County Clare." The young gentleman grinned and reached a hand to Liam. "I'm Charlie Schweinfurth, from Cayuga County, New York, but I guess I have to rethink that pronunciation. This is Cuyahoga County, now, right?"

"Yes, sir," Liam smiled. "Euclid Township in Cuyahoga County. Home of the finest bluestone this side of the Mississippi."

"A salesman, Charlie. Watch your step." Schweinfurth's companion chuckled and extended a hand toward Liam. "I'm Charlie's brother J. A."

"Sir," Liam shook his hand, then turned back to the stone piled outside the shed. "This is the finished stone, foundation stone here," Liam gestured, "and cladding stone, and over there some lintel stone. We don't do much of the smaller stone, except sidewalk flagging. Ours is mostly structural. This rail line should be finished by fall, and then we'll be able to get the stone to the city a lot faster. We ship by the wagonload."

"And yours is one of the group?" Charlie Schweinfurth asked.

"It is, sir. My team can haul a ton-and-a-half easy."

"J. A., how far do you think we are from Everett's property? Ten, fifteen mile?" Charlie asked.

"Something like that. A good bit of it is downhill, though." J. A. turned to Liam. "Have you hauled stone into Cleveland?"

"Not all the way in, sir. Doan's Corners is as far as I've gone. Some big homes going up near there. I've taken in some cladding stone."

The Schweinfurth brothers were roaming among the stone blocks, outside the shed and inside, running their hands over the edges, inspecting the grain and colors.

"Donovan, what kind of foundation stones have you hauled nearby?" Charlie asked.

"Well, sir, the Methodists are building a church up the road some. We're taking foundation stone there starting on Monday."

The two men exchanged bright glances. "Could we come along, Donovan? I'd like to see how this bluestone sits in Cayuga—I mean, Cuyahoga soil."

Just at dawn on Monday morning, Liam was loading his wagon with the foundation stones. It was fine stone, grey with just a hint of blue, and a speckled, wispy grain

that reminded Liam of midmorning clouds. The wagon had once belonged to his Da. Matt Donovan had worked at the quarry until three years ago when his left leg was crushed under a collapsed side wall. After his Da's accident, Liam had inherited his job along with the wooden wagon to haul the stone. The wagon was a sturdy four-wheeled vehicle with its own built-in pulley system, making it easy to hoist the heavy bluestone. As usual, Gustaf Lindstrom, a stocky blond nineteen-year-old, was helping Liam slide a thick chain underneath each of the stones, and together they used the pulley to raise it into the wagon bed. The wood creaked under the weight of the slabs.

Once the wagon was fully loaded, Liam hitched up his horses, Sean and Seamus, to the harness tree. Matt Donovan had bought these two chestnuts almost ten years earlier, and they had known and responded to Matt as if they could read his mind. It had taken Liam more than a year—and a good number of sugar cubes—to persuade them to work as his own team, not his father's. Ornery as usual, the stubborn geldings tossed their heads against the harness and collars. Liam patted Seamus's flank, the color of shiny buckeyes that fell each October. "Don't worry, fellas. It ain't a far haul," he whispered. Beside him, Sean snorted. Laughing, Liam hopped into the cart beside Gus. With a flick of the reins, they started moving.

Liam steered his team south toward the Plank Road. Gus started humming one of those lilting Swedish folk tunes Liam loved to hear.

The day promised to be a beautiful one. Springtime, thought Liam, was the best season—crisp, sweet air, budding gardens, and folk cheerful to be out of winter's chill.

As the quarrymen passed the Donovan house on their way to the site, Liam marveled at how tiny the house seemed from the outside, much too small to hold his family of seven—three of them little ones. His mouth quirked into a smile at the thought of his rambunctious younger siblings. No doubt Stephen and Jamie were finishing their chores for Ma or Da before school. And his sister Katie, not so little anymore, was already off to work at Mr. Scheide's restaurant on the Plank Road.

It took Liam and Gus about a half hour to reach the Plank Road, where Liam urged his team right onto the planks, hundreds of wooden slabs wedged into the earth, taking travelers out of mud from the city out to the Chagrin river valley on the east. The horses clopped the short distance to the church site, which wasn't too far from the corner.

There the Methodists had already dug a deep hole and framed it with sturdy wooden boards set vertically into the ground, looking like an underground fence. The hole would eventually become the church's cellar, and with the wooden frame, the bluestone slabs would provide a strong foundation for the new church building.

Hopping down from the seat, Gus tended to the stones, while Liam tended to his team. From his pocket he pulled a couple of fresh carrots, snapped them into bite-sized halves, cupped them in his palms, and offered them to the horses. Sean and Seamus eagerly devoured them, their lips tickling Liam's fingers.

Mr. Manning was already there, standing near the excavation with a small cluster of men. Among them were the Schweinfurth brothers, pointing at the hole and discussing its depth, along with the Methodist parson, Reverend Tagg, one of the Methodist circuit riders who travelled between different churches to preach. No doubt he had made a special trip from his church in Nottingham village to be present when the foundation to this new building was to be laid.

"G'morning, sirs!" Liam said, raising a hand in greeting once his horses were finished.

"Morning, Donovan." J.A. and Charlie met the boys at the wagon, eager to see the process from beginning to end. "Show us how you Cuyahoga folks lay a foundation."

"We'll do our best, sir," Liam grinned. Using the chain from his wagon's pulley, Liam and Gus started to unload the bluestone slabs.

"How much would you say one of those stones weighs, Donovan?" Charlie asked.

"Near about two-hundred and fifty pound, sir," Liam said.

"And how much can your team haul in a day?"

"A ton and a half, sir. That's usually ten stones like these," Liam said, pride coloring his voice.

Liam and Gus set to work. They lowered the cornerstones in first, as they were the most important ones. Other stones could be trimmed to fit inside that framing as needed. Standing inside the excavation with two of the Methodist workmen, Liam steadied the stones as Gus lowered them, the stones smooth and cool against his palms. As the side stones were placed against the wooden framing, the workmen sealed them in place with thick cold mortar made of lime, water, and sand.

Every few minutes one of the Schweinfurth brothers would ask them about the stones, or the mortar, the pulley, never running out of questions. Liam and Gus answered them as best they could. They explained how the grain of the rock made the stones look attractive, and how sometimes the grain was horizontal and thin as a spider's web. They explained how the foundation stones should be thick enough to provide support, but not too thick that they'd crack. They explained how the smooth texture of the stone sometimes made it hard to handle. As they worked and talked, the sun climbed, heating the May morning till it felt more like July. Shortly before midday, Liam and Gus headed back to the quarry for the second load, eating their bread-and-cheese sandwiches on the way.

The afternoon wore on in the routine of lifting, setting, mortaring and tamping the stone into the foundation walls. When the sun was low and their shadows stretched long, Gus and Liam swept the last of the straw from the back of the wagon, and readied the team to head home. When they looked at the site one last time, they saw that Charlie and J.A. were deep in conversation with Mr. Manning. They climbed into the wagon, and Liam took the reins.

"Donovan! Lindstrom!" It was Mr. Manning. Liam and Gus exchanged glances, but jumped from the wagon and walked back to their boss and the Schweinfurth brothers.

"Boys," J.A. said brightly, "my brother and I are very impressed with your skills. We need folks who know the stone."

"How would you two like to come work for us at the Everett site?" Charlie asked.

"You mean in the city, sir?" Liam said.

"Over on Case avenue at Euclid," Charlie nodded. "We already discussed it with Manning, and he's agreed to spare you for the next few months."

Liam was speechless. After a pause, he said, "I'm honored for the opportunity, sir. But I'd like to talk it over with my father."

J.A. nodded. "Sure thing, Donovan."

"We're heading back into the city on Wednesday," Charlie said. "We'd like to have your decision by tomorrow."

They drove slowly back to the quarry, where Liam would drop Gus off for his walk to his boarding house on the Bluestone road. All along the way, Liam listened while Gus chattered on gaily about this chance to work with the Schweinfurths, to move into the city, to be off on his own. Liam nodded, smiled when he could, and finally said good-bye to his friend.

He was glad for the solitude on the final mile toward his own house. He weighed the possibility. To work in the city would be a great opportunity, and working with one of the finest young architects in the country would be hard to pass up. If the Everett site was a dozen miles away, he could never go and come back and still do a day's work. He guessed he'd earn more with the Schweinfurths than at the quarry. But could he abandon his responsibility to his family? His Da was able to work at the house, repairing harness for Mr. Albright's saddlery, but his earnings from piecework couldn't support the family. Katie's earnings at the restaurant weren't much. Could they survive without him?

After tending to the horses—unhitching, grooming, watering and feeding Sean and Seamus, and latching the barn door—Liam did a quick wash at the pump beside the trough before entering the house. He was weighing his words, trying to find a way to describe Mr. Schweinfurth's offer without leaning one way or the other.

Taking a deep breath, he squared his shoulders and climbed the three stone steps to the kitchen.

"Ah, Liam! 'Tis yourself at last!" Ellen Donovan was at the stove, stirring the soup, her reddish-blonde braids wound round her head, and her usual warm smile lighting her face.

"It is, Ma." Liam gave her a kiss and turned to the sink, pumping water to wash his hands again.

"How did the foundation turn out?" his father called from the chair near the front window. Though he could no longer work at the quarry, Matt Donovan still prided himself on his knowledge of the stone, and kept up to date on the quarry's work through his eldest.

"It was good, Da," Liam answered, replacing the towel behind the sink and taking his seat at the dinner table. "Mr. Manning let Gus and me handle it. The men from the church had a good cellar dug, and the stones fit well."

"Good measuring, ye and that Swede," Matt smiled. "I'm proud of ye, m'boy."

Ellen brought the soup pot to the table, and Liam's sister Katie brought the platter of bread and the butter crock. After their simple grace, the family settled in to the potato and onion soup, listening to ten-year-old Stephen and seven-year-old Jamie describe what they had learned at the Stone schoolhouse. Ellen tempted baby Mary with bits of bread and small bits of potato. Katie had little to tell from her day at Mr. Scheide's restaurant on the Plank Road; nothing more than the usual hay farmers and dairymen making their way toward the market at the Warrensville road and back.

When their bowls were empty, and the younger boys had finished second pieces of buttered bread, Katie cleared the bowls while her mother brought the pan of baked apples from the oven. As a treat this bright spring evening, Ellen brought a small pitcher of cream as well, to pour over the warm dessert. Liam swallowed hard, and stepped into the quiet.

"Ma, Da, do you remember last week when I told you about the architects from New York who were talking at the quarry with Mr. Manning? They were at the church site today, watching us set the foundation." Liam looked at each of his parents in turn, but they were enjoying their dessert, it seemed, only half paying attention to him.

It was Katie who seemed to be hearing something out of the ordinary in Liam's story. "Is New York stonework different from Euclid Township stonework?" she asked.

"Well, no, not really," Liam said slowly, glancing again at his parents, who now were more alert. "Mr. Schweinfurth, the main one, he has done some building at Washington, near the Capitol, and he has a contract to build a house at Euclid avenue for a banker, and he likes the bluestone in Mr. Manning's shed, and he likes the way Gus and me were handling the stone today, and he asked if Gus and me, and if Mr. Manning, well, if we might be interested in working at the banker's house site starting this summer."

Liam felt as if his lungs were empty. All he could hear was the early evening breeze lifting the curtains at the window. Stephen and Jamie stared at him, their eyes darting between their parents' faces for some response. Matt and Ellen looked at one another, saying nothing.

Finally Katie spoke. "So you'd have to live in the city, not here." It was a statement more than a question.

Liam swallowed hard.

His mother echoed Katie's question. "Ye'd not be living here?"

Matt looked hard at his first-born child. "Ye'd be after earning more with this architect than ye would with Manning, am I right?"

"Yes, sir."

The silence in the room deepened.

"Liam, ye are a good lad, a good young man, to be thinking of your family," Ellen spoke slowly. "If this opportunity is one that will be a good one, then I think ye should do what ye need to do." She looked long at him, and Liam smiled a bit.

"Thanks, Ma," he said quietly. He looked at his father, who returned his steady gaze. It was enough. "Thank you, Da."

Matt nodded solemnly.

"I'll sleep on it, and pray on it, and let you know in the morning," Liam said softly, and put his spoon into his baked apple.

The sky was still grey when Liam hauled himself out of bed. Although reciting his nighttime prayers had given him some peace, it had still been a sleepless night. Jamie and Stephen slept hard and soundlessly next to him, but Liam had spent hours watching the stars, and the flutter of the curtain at the window. Now he sat on the edge of the bed, his brothers still snoring. He took a slow breath.

Rubbing the tiredness from his eyes, he pulled on his shirt, tugged on his trousers, and clasped his suspenders before sliding on boots, lacing them up, and heading downstairs. He headed to the little barn behind the house to give Sean and Seamus their morning bags of oats.

"Do you think I'm making the right choice, boys?" Liam said, brushing Seamus's mane out of his eyes before hitching the feedbag over his ears.

"You think too much," a voice behind him said. Liam turned to find Katie in the doorway of the barn, holding the water pitcher that Ma had sent her out to fill.

Liam's face tightened. "I just don't want to leave you all here to fend for yourselves."

Katie sniffed. "I make a decent sum working at the restaurant. Even if it is just washing and cleaning," she said, with a gentle smile. 'I want the best for you, Liam. Ma and Da, too. So, don't go beating yourself up over this."

"Thanks, Katie."

After breakfast, after many more hugs than usual from his Ma and little siblings, Liam hitched up his team and headed to the quarry. The Schweinfurth brothers were already there, chatting with Mr. Manning outside the shed, their hats tilted back on their heads.

"There you are, Donovan!" J.A. said, waving him over. Liam hopped down from the wagon, patting Sean on the flank before walking over to the brothers. His stomach was air. He felt like he was standing at the edge of a cliff. "G'morning, sirs."

"So, lad, have you made up your mind?" Charlie asked. "Will you be coming with us to the Everett site?"

Liam straightened, and his smile stretched into a grin. "Yes, sir, I will."

J.A. beamed at him, and Charlie reached out to shake Liam's hand. "That's great news, Donovan," Charlie said. "Welcome to the team."

It Was Worth It:
A Story of South Euclid in 1915

The man in the ticket booth stared them down, his eyes narrowed with skepticism. George's heart beat hard and his nerve started to evaporate. The hand holding his coins was just as sweaty as the one inside his baseball glove; both were trembling. His stomach did an uneasy shuffle, along with his feet. After making it all this way, would they now be turned away at the very gate of League Park?

The man did not avert his gaze, but the boys did. Billy, Carl, and George looked at the ground for fear that their eyes would betray their consciences. Could this man see right through them and all their carefully concocted lies?

Then, his gaze still incredulous, the ticket man asked the one question they had feared.

"Aren't you boys supposed to be in school?"

* * *

George Henderson spat in his baseball glove and looked toward the gravel path leading up to the white frame house. He and his pals, Carl Larsen and Billy Schiltz, had been helping out on Nap's farm since school let out in June. Now they were waiting for him to come home so they could play catch.

Mr. Napoleon "Nap" Lajoie was one of the best players for the Naps, Cleveland's major-league baseball team. His farm was on Mayfield road just east of town. After school, George and his friends sometimes helped with chores on the farm until Mr. Lajoie came home. (Most of all George liked to feed the chickens.) Then Nap would play catch with the boys for a time.

There was no doubt that Nap was a great baseball player. In 1901, he had won the American League Triple Crown, and since coming to play for the Cleveland club in 1902, he had led the team to steady success. This summer he was on pace to get his 3000th hit. Fearless Nap! George wanted to be just like Mr. Lajoie when he grew up.

The shadows were getting long under the trees when they heard the clang of the red interurban car. Looking out toward Mayfield road, the boys saw Nap leap down from the car, wave his cap to the driver, and sprint up the gravel road toward them. In a crowd, Mr. Lajoie was hard to miss. He was very tall with a long face, just right for intimidating his opponents. His sharp brown eyes reminded you of a tiger staring you down, perfect for knowing the exact moment to swing the bat or the exact place to catch a pop fly. And then there were his large ears. George guessed that these were *not* so perfect for blocking out boos from the crowd, but probably aided him in keeping his balance when he was up at bat.

Sometimes, when Mr. Lajoie had a serious expression on his face, deep lines would form between his thin cheeks and his even thinner lips. In the front of his baseball cap, sometimes a small tuft of hair stuck out. Although he knew it was silly, George imagined a plant growing on top of Nap's head.

George rarely saw Nap's serious expression, however. When he came home, Mr. Lajoie was almost always in a good mood and he loved playing catch with the boys, as he did now.

No sooner had Nap reached the porch and hung his suit jacket over the railing than he threw the first pitch. George liked to play catch with Nap. When they played together, George almost felt as if *he* were a player in the American league, too! Sometimes Mrs. Lajoie would bring out grapes and cookies for them, and Mr. Lajoie would tell the children stories of his hometown, Woonsocket, Rhode Island.

Some days, Mrs. Lajoie would watch their game from the back porch while she sliced strawberries or cored apples. George thought Mrs. Lajoie was very pretty. Her hair reminded George of calming waves on the ocean. Her voice was like waves, too. George liked to hear her talk. She made all her words sound long and lazy.

"Now, boys, y'all run on home! We don't want your mamas worrying about you!" she would smile.

The boys always replied in chorus: "Yes, ma'am."

"And, Nap, your supper's getting cold!"

She'd give the boys one last smile as she turned to go back to her kitchen.

That was last year.

And this was this year - 1915. May 15, 1915, to be exact.

George was sitting on a bench in Mr. Kirby's coal yard, throwing lumps of coal at the wall of the storage shed. This was his favorite place in the world to sit and think, the best place in the world.

George was thinking about Mr. Lajoie. He stopped throwing coal and reached into his pocket. He pulled out the *Lucky Hit* baseball cards he had got at Mr. Bilkey's confectionery store, and started shuffling through them. Each face stared up at him: Ray Chapman (shortstop), Elmer Smith (outfield), and "Shoeless" Joe Jackson, all part of the 1915 Cleveland club. The Indians. George was still getting used to the nickname. Just a year ago the team had been The Cleveland Naps, in honor of Mr. Nap Lajoie himself. But Nap got traded to the Philadelphia Athletics, so the team was called the Indians now.

As great as they were, Chapman, Smith, and Jackson couldn't compare to George's favorite baseball player of all: Mr. Napoleon Lajoie. George missed playing catch with Nap and Carl and Billy. Nap had such a good arm! What an adventure it would be to actually see Nap play. In a real baseball game. Maybe see Chapman, Smith, and Jackson on the diamond at League Park.

George snapped out of his daydream and chortled at this impossibly impossible idea. What was he thinking? Where would he get the money to get into the ball park? And how would he get there? Still, it would be a nice alternative to Miss Geiger droning on and on about arithmetic and direct objects, and . . .

Suddenly, it was as if a bolt of lightning came down and struck George right on the noodle. He stood up, dropping his baseball cards. He had just devised the cleverest scheme to get to see Nap again, and this time, in action! No fourteen-year-old boy had ever devised such a clever plan, which was to be expected. George was certainly the cleverest, craftiest boy in the township's brand new brick schoolhouse. (No one could deny that that spider trick he played on rotten old know-it-all Gertrude Eleanor Hofmeier was anything short of cunning. She had gotten it, all right!)

But that was then. This was now. Now, he felt all the cunning of a fox. Now, George Donald Henderson had a plan, a plan that required the slyness of a fox with a baseball glove.

* * *

George could hardly wait for Monday to tell his friends of his brilliant scheme. As soon as school let out, he caught sight of Carl and Billy, but they weren't alone. Tagging alongside them was Carl's little brother Frankie. Just five years old, Frankie had freckles and blond hair, like most of the Larsen family. Carl had to watch his brother after school nearly every day because their mother had a brand new baby at home and she didn't want Frankie underfoot any more than necessary. Frankie was all right, for a little kid, except that he was a tattle-tale. If someone did something bad or went somewhere they weren't supposed to, Frank would be sure to tell the adults. George knew they had to find a way to keep Frankie from finding out about their scheme and telling his parents. They had to find a way to keep Frankie's mouth shut.

"Hey, fellas," said George, smiling broadly—maybe too broadly.

Billy and Carl looked at him skeptically. They could tell George was up to something. It was written all over his face.

"Carl! ... Carl! ... CARL!" demanded Frankie.

"What?" replied Carl.

"Can we go over to Mr. Bilkey's and get some Mary Janes?"

"No, Frankie. You don't need that..." said Carl, taking a deep breath, clearly annoyed.

Frankie's lower lip began to stretch into its familiar pout before he stomped off to climb the school steps so he could jump off the low stone wall, over and over, airing his aggravation. They let him go. As long as Carl could keep Frankie in view, they could make their plans in peace.

"I was sitting in Mr. Kirby's coal yard for a long time on Saturday. I miss playing ball with Nap, don't you?" The other boys nodded, and Carl threw a stone against a tree trunk. "So I think we should go to one of Nap's games. The Athletics are coming to Cleveland to play at the end of the month. What do you say we go to a game?"

"How are we going to get there?" Carl asked. "League Park is all the way in town."

"I have it all planned out," George said. "The Indians play the Athletics on Monday, May 24th."

"But that's a school day," Billy complained.

"What's more important, Billy Schiltz? Miss Geiger or Napoleon Lajoie?"

Billy was silent.

"All right. First thing, general admission to the game is seventy-five cents." George checked each boy's response: tense, but reasonably tense. "To get there, we take the C & E, but it'll cost us each thirty cents each way."

"Thirty cents!" Billy burst out. "Where am I going to get another thirty cents!"

"And a penny for a transfer to the Euclid car. Twice. So it'll be sixty-two cents each."

Billy's mouth was open. "How ... but ..."

"Listen. We take the C & E to town, transfer to the Euclid car, ride to East 70th, and then we walk to the ball park. It's easy. We've got a week and a half to get the money. We can do extra chores, and I guess stay away from Mr. Bilkey's for a while. If we have enough, we can buy something to eat at the park." George looked from Carl to Billy. "What do you say, fellows? Are you in?"

Billy and Carl exchanged glances.

"I'm in," said Carl, swallowing hard.

"Me, too," Billy agreed. "This is going to be swell!"

The boys all put their hands in, just as Nap said his teammates did before a game. Just then, they noticed that Frankie had come up alongside of them. He had watched and heard every detail of the plan.

"Frankie! We're just talking. There's nothing important here. Don't you dare tell Mother and Father a word of this!" Carl sounded desperate. "I'll . . . I'll take you over to Mr. Bilkey's. Come on. I can get you five Mary Janes as long as you don't say a word about this to Mother and Father. Promise?"

"All right. But it has to be Mary Janes. You really promise? Then I won't tell a word!" agreed Frankie.

As Carl and Frankie headed toward Mayfield road, George and Billy turned north for home. As long as Frankie kept quiet, and as long as they could all find enough money, their plan was in motion to get to League Park and see their hero, Nap Lajoie, one more time.

* * *

George, Billy and Carl met in the schoolyard, as usual, with baseball mitts, on the morning of Monday, May 24. Except they had no schoolbooks in straps today, just the mitts. They were anxious, and about twenty minutes early. While the other children talked and played around them, the boys played catch for a while, then raced each other to Mayfield road and back of couple of times, but the last sprint took them across the road and the railroad tracks to Mr. Kirby's coal yard, behind the shed. They emptied their pockets into George's cap and counted the money.

"Five dollars and forty-seven cents. That'll get us there and back," George announced. His cap was heavy. He liked the feel of it. He'd never had that much money in one place before.

"All right, fellows," Carl said. "Everybody take thirty cents and a penny for the trip to town." The boys selected their coins. "Now another thirty-one cents for everybody." More selecting and pocketing. "And seventy-five cents each for the ticket to the game." More selecting. "What's left, George?"

"A dollar and thirty-six cents. We still have enough for some peanuts and a scorecard, and maybe a root beer."

They laughed, enjoying the freedom and adventure of it. And then they heard the clang of the school bell across the street. They grew quiet. It was official: they were playing hooky. And they were on their way to see Nap Lajoie at League Park.

 With their coins in their pockets and lumps in their throats, the boys slipped from behind the shed and made for the Green road intersection. As the big red car rattled to a stop, the boys climbed aboard and handed over their fares. They sat together on one caned seat, carefully pocketing their paper transfers, nervous about skipping school but glad that they were actually so close to seeing Nap. As the C & E car moved westward, they passed the Lutheran church, hayfields and strawberry farms, and cow pastures.

"Look!" Billy pointed. "There's Al Prasse's farm!"

They passed more dairy farms, and white wooden houses very much like their own. Then they began to notice enormous houses built of stone and brick, set deep behind vast green lawns and stone walls. When the tracks swung left, and then right, they saw tall brick buildings on both sides of the road, four stories high, with rows of windows and front porches on each floor. The car lurched right again and began to go downhill, revealing to the boys a panorama of the whole city of Cleveland, and beyond, the blue of the lake meeting the blue of the sky. They were on their way.

When the C & E car reached Euclid Avenue, the boys alighted on the street, clutching their transfers. All around them, book-toting boys not much older than they, in flannel trousers and big, loose ties, were hurrying across the tree-shaded lawns of Adelbert College. In just a few minutes, the Euclid avenue streetcar came along. The boys climbed in, handed over their transfers, and watched as the college grounds slid past.

Once they were settled on the streetcar, they knew they were only minutes away from seeing their hero. The sun was moving higher in the summer-like sky. The people around them in the streetcar, mostly men in suits and stiff collars and straw hats, were reading their newspapers, not noticing the boys. That made them feel relieved. The only other children in the car were toddlers with their mothers. Billy and Carl were feeling worried, but George assured them that things were fine, that boys their age rode the cars all the time.

Finally, the car reached the stop at East 70th street. The boys climbed off the car and immediately started walking north, single file behind George, just like they always did in the schoolyard. The street was shady and breezy, the houses much closer together than out in the township. Only a few people were on the street, and they could hear small children playing in their yards and on their porches. Walking quickly, the boys crossed Hough avenue, then Quimby avenue, and finally reached Lexington. They stood and looked at each other, and at the concrete and wood structure in front of them. League Park. They had arrived.

The Lexington avenue sidewalk was packed with men jostling one another. The boys edged their way through the crowd toward the ticket booth, nervously jingling the coins in their pockets. As they got closer to the booth, their anxiety mounted. George was chewing the inside of his cheek, twisting his handkerchief in his pocket. He was feeling really short, surrounded by crowds of adults. Catching Carl's eye, he guessed Carl was feeling pretty much the same.

When they finally got to the ticket booth, Billy was first. He handed over his seventy-five cents, but the man looked sternly at all three boys.

"Aren't you boys supposed to be in school?"

Billy froze.

"No, sir," George croaked. "We have the day off. We're here to see Nap Lajoie play ball!" The other boys smiled and nodded tightly, watching the ticket man's face. To their amazement, he smiled.

"His uniform may say *Philadelphia*, but Napoleon Lajoie will always be Cleveland's number one player." He took their coins, handed them three tickets, and waved them through the turnstile.

They were in the clear. In relief, they grinned, and began threading their way through the crowd, heading toward the right field grandstand. Up the cement ramps they walked, still nervous, but the noise of so many people talking, and the smell of popcorn in the air, turned their anxiety into genuine excitement.

At the top of the ramp, the boys found themselves rooted to the floor. They were at the top of an aisle, and below in front of them was the outfield, as rich and bright a green as their eyes had ever beheld. And there, out on the grass, were the Philadelphia Athletics, playing catch and running, hitting one another ground balls and fly balls, just as Mr. Lajoie had played with them on the farm just last summer.

They leaped down the concrete steps two at a time, darting to the railing to scan the faces of the men on the field. And sure enough, George spotted his hero's unmistakable face: those ears, that tuft of hair peeking up from under the bill of his cap.

"Mr. Lajoie! Mr. Lajoie!" the boys called, waving wildly.

Nap turned toward the stands, letting his bat rest on his shoulder as he squinted in the sunshine to see who had called him.

"Mr. Lajoie! It's us, Billy and Carl and George!"

And to their amazed delight, Napoleon Lajoie, star second baseman of the American League Champion Philadelphia Athletics, trotted over to the right field railing. "Hey, boys! Good to see you! I guess you remember your old neighbor!"

For the next few minutes, the three boys chatted with Nap, clutching their mitts while their hero tapped his bat on his shoulder, his face crinkled in the smile they remembered so well. Then it was time for the teams to start the game, so Nap solemnly shook hands with Billy, and Carl, and George, tipped his cap to them, and trotted back toward the A's dugout. As they stood at the rail, the boys had nothing to say. No words were worth spending any breath on. They could see Nap blend into the knot of gray-clad players clustered around Mr. Mack near first base, and the Cleveland players gathered around Mr. Fohl beyond third. Slowly they turned to find their seats.

"Hey, fellows. Let's enjoy this game! And let's spend this money while we have it. What do you say?" George exclaimed.

"I'll get some peanuts," Billy said. "Carl, what about some root beer?"

George dug the rest of their money out of his left pocket. "I'll get us a scorecard. I want us to remember this game as long as we live."

Just under the shade of the grandstand roof, the boys munched happily on the peanuts, and even bought a box of Cracker Jack to share. It wasn't much of a lunch, but with the root beer they had all they needed for a fine afternoon. They cheered wildly whenever Nap came to the plate, and applauded his every catch and assist at second base. When the Indians were in the field, they called out to Shoeless Joe in the outfield, and politely jeered at Jack Hammond, who had no right to be playing second base for Cleveland—that should be Nap's place. As the bottom of the ninth inning wound down, the Cleveland team was unable to get the fifth run to tie the game, so the Indians lost again. But the boys weren't too disappointed: their hero's team had won.

The players drifted into their dugouts as the crowd filed out of the park, marching slowly up the cement steps toward the concourse and the exits. The boys sat in their seats, watching the scoreboard numbers and the flags come down.

"I guess we should head home," George sighed, gently rubbing his mitt.

"We're going to be in trouble, aren't we?" Billy asked bleakly.

"At school and at home," Carl groaned. "What a way to end the year."

"Yeah, but still," George said, "wasn't it worth it? Aren't you glad we came?"

The three of them sat a few moments longer, memorizing the color of the grass and the angles of the light, smelling the hot iron and cement around them, and the salt of the popcorn and peanuts that still hung in the air.

"Yeah. It was worth it. It was definitely worth it."

Finding the Courage:
A Story of South Euclid in 1925

Milena Doubek trudged out of the Green Road School, trying to swallow the lump that had formed in her throat. Her arms wound around her textbook, hugging its tattered cover tight against her chest. She glanced back at the two-story brick building, the afternoon sun  reflecting off the school's windows, which peered down at her like the watchful eyes of her eighth-grade teacher. The lump in her throat got bigger, and Milena quickly averted her eyes to the sidewalk.

Milena was jolted when Elenora Moretti lightly bumped into her with her shoulder. "Cheer up, Lena. I'm sure it won't be *that* bad." Elenora held her own book by its spine, swinging it a little as she walked. Milena marveled at her friend's apparent lack of care.

"Elenora's right. It's just an elocution assignment," Emily Greene, another of their friends, said reassuringly, coming alongside them.

Milena's grip tightened on her book. "Elocution sounds like *electrocution.* And I'll bet it's just as painful, too!" she sighed.

Emily laughed at that. "Elocution is just public speaking. And we only have to recite one speech! There's nothing to be scared of."

Milena lowered her eyes, studying the bluestone sidewalk beneath her feet as they walked toward Mayfield road. "It might not be scary for you, but I *hate* public speaking. When I get in front of people, I start shaking and my stomach starts to hurt and I start talking really fast in this high pitched voice and I forget what to say and I—"

"*Smettere*! Just stop right there. *Smettere*!" Elenora laughed. "You're only making yourself more nervous."

"Say, I have an idea," Emily broke in. "Why don't you practice in front of the children at Rainbow, Milena? It would be a great way to overcome your stage fright."

"Good idea! Maybe I'll practice my speech for them, too," Elenora said.

"You'll have to write it, first," Emily chuckled. "Do you have any ideas?"

"Not yet." The warm September wind tousled her hair, blowing a couple of dark strands into her eyes. Elenora blew them out of the way, but they fell back over her face moments later. "Ugh! How *fastidivo!* So annoying! Maybe I'll cut my hair again."

"Again? You'll have a bob if you keep this up." Emily sounded stunned.

"That movie star Marion Davies has a bob, and she's the bee's knees," Elenora said.

"At least wait until after this weekend to chop off all your hair. What if it looks awful on you? You don't want to look bad for the Forty Hours procession this weekend," Milena said.

They were walking past St. Gregory's new white frame church, which faced Emily's Methodist church across the street.

"I'm so excited that I can come with you two this year!" Emily bubbled.

The parish was not yet five years old, but Forty Hours was already an annual event at St. Gregory's. Held every year on the weekend closest to the September 3 feast of St. Gregory, Forty Hours brought people to church for quiet prayer, services, adoration, and a closing procession with benediction. Emily, a Methodist, wouldn't be attending the service itself, but she had received permission from her family to attend the social afterwards. It had taken some convincing, though. Her father had finally agreed, but not before muttering for a while about *those Catholics.*

"I don't mind if my hair ends up looking awful. It'll give our parents something to complain about besides Antonio and Irena," Elenora said.

Milena winced a little at that. Milena's older sister Irena was keeping company with Antonio, Elenora's older brother. They were a sweet couple, Emily always said, and Elenora and Milena quietly agreed. But Mr. Doubek and Mr. Moretti would never approve, so Antonio and Irena tried mightily to keep it a secret from their families. Italians and Bohemians being *friends* was one thing, but a *couple*? That was inexcusable in their fathers' eyes.

"Forty Hours will sure be interesting," Milena agreed, frowning at the thought of her father's temper. "I'm just excited about all the food that will be there. My mother's making *kolache,* these little fruit cookies. My mother is the best cook in South Euclid."

Elenora scoffed. "The best? Never! Just wait until you try *my* mother's *cannoli.*"

An idea popped into Milena's head. "Say, do you think I could do my speech on making *kolache?* Sort of a how-to speech?" It would certainly be easy to speak about something she knew so well, Milena reasoned.

Emily looped an arm around her friend's waist. "I think that's a fantastic idea," she grinned.

The three girls strolled the rest of the way to Rainbow, laughing and teasing and enjoying the afternoon sunshine. When they reached the tall frame house that was Rainbow Hospital for Crippled Children, the girls

followed the path around to the back of the building, under the shade of a grove of tall maples. Climbing the steep wooden steps to the back door, they slipped inside. Stopping in the kitchen to say hello to Elenora's mother, Mrs. Moretti, they went through the dining room to the sunny front room which was the Bingham School classroom.

This was the girls' routine, every day after school, visiting the children at the Rainbow Hospital. All of their mothers worked there, Mrs. Moretti in the kitchen, Mrs. Doubek in the laundry along with her daughter Irena, while Mrs. Greene was a part of the nursing staff. The girls would linger at the hospital until their parents finished their shifts and all went home. Sometimes the girls would help Mrs. Moretti chop vegetables, or fold the children's shirts and drawers with Mrs. Doubek, but more often they would just sit and visit with the children.

Last year the school district had opened a school, the Bingham School at Rainbow, enabling the children to keep up with their learning while they recovered from operations or sickness. Though the children were in various grades, Emily, Elenora and Milena still found ways to study with all of them. Milena especially liked teaching the younger children some of the more advanced arithmetic. She loved hearing about how they showed off their newfound knowledge to their teacher, Miss Haigh.

When Milena and her friends entered the classroom, the children's faces lit up. They were children of different backgrounds: German and Irish, Bohemian and Swedish, Italian and Jewish—all born in Cleveland, all Americans. Unlike some of their parents, these children had no problem befriending each other, enjoying one another's company, especially here, away from their own families.

"What did you do in school today?" Elenora asked the group happily.

Annmarie, a tiny eight-year-old with blonde pigtails, replied. "We went over our times tables, and I got almost all of them right! Miss Haigh says I'm one of her best third-graders!"

"That's *stupendo*, Annmarie! Just wonderful! Remember last month, when you could barely do three times four?" Elenora smiled, pulling up a chair next to Annmarie's wheelchair.

Annmarie's little chest puffed up with pride. The other children all chimed in with their latest academic accomplishments.

"Could you all do us a favor today?" Emily asked. "The three of us have an elocution assignment, and we want to practice in front of you."

The children perked up in excitement, and little Annmarie clapped. "Yes, yes! I'm a very good listener. Mamma always says so."

"You have to be hard on us," Elenora warned. "You have to all tell us if we stutter, or start to talk too fast or anything. We're counting on you."

The children nodded their heads in solemn agreement. The three girls clustered with the convalescent children, chattering about topic sentences, specific details, transitions and conclusions. When each of them had an outline, they got up in front of the group to practice. Elenora spoke first, giving her presentation almost flawlessly, describing the children's own Bingham School. Annmarie, Martin and Eddie were delighted when Elenora mentioned them by name. Emily spoke next, doing her speech on the dangers of automobiles like the Model T Ford. She stumbled a bit over some of the technical terms about automobile machinery, but those were the parts the boys especially liked, about tires and crankshafts and carburetors.

Finally it was Milena's turn, and as she stood in front of her friends she could feel her heart hammering against her ribcage. Her first attempt was breathy and stumbling; it was such a disaster that Elenora made her stop in the middle and start over.

"I can't help it! You're all staring at me, and it makes me so *nervózní*!"

"Try looking above our heads, instead of at us directly. Maybe your nerves won't be as bad," Emily suggested.

Milena took a calming breath, and tried again. Staring at the fireplace behind the children seemed to help. After a few more attempts, and with more guidance from Elenora, Emily, and the children, Milena fell into a rhythm, reciting her speech with near-perfect articulation. When she finished, the little ones burst into applause, and Eddie begged her to bring *kolache* with her tomorrow afternoon. Milena gave a little curtsey, red-faced but pleased.

"Thank you all so much for listening to us practice," Elenora said, as she and her friends prepared to leave the schoolroom. "We'll see you tomorrow. You better get *all* your times tables right tomorrow, Annmarie!"

The girls went their own ways, then, Elenora to the kitchen, and Emily to the upstairs ward where her mother worked. Brimming with confidence, Milena went out back to the laundry building where her mother and Irena would be finishing up the last of their work. Arriving in the main wash room, Milena found Irena alone, ironing. "Mamma's in the drying room, collecting more clean sheets," Irena said, answering Milena's unasked question.

Seeing Mrs. Doubek's absence as an opportunity, Milena pounced. "So how is Antonio?" she asked with a sly grin, pulling a stool up to the ironing board. She rarely missed an opportunity to tease her sister, and her success with her speech had made her bold.

Pink crept onto Irena's cheeks. "He's taking me to the pictures next Friday, at the Woodman Hall," she said. It was no wonder that Antonio was interested in Irena: at seventeen, Irena was beautiful, with long, gentle limbs, a creamy complexion, dark brown hair-- almost black, and a softness about her face that Milena had always envied. "I like him so much, Lena," Irena whispered. "Antonio is so *hodný*, so gentle and considerate."

Milena glanced at the doorway, making sure her mother was not nearby. "What are you going to do when Papa finds out? He's bound to see you and Antonio together at the social after Forty Hours."

"I don't know," Irena confessed. She frowned down at the pillow slip in front of her, changing the iron, gliding the hot one across the wrinkles with measured, practiced strokes. "You know, I'm almost glad for Forty Hours. I'm tired of hiding from Papa and making up stories when I want to see Antonio. And who knows? Papa might not mind."

Milena sniffed skeptically. *That* was unlikely. But then Mrs. Doubek came back into the room with an armload of sheets, and that was the end of the conversation.

At school the following day, Milena's big moment arrived. Since her teacher called the eighth-graders in alphabetical order, Milena was among the first to do her speech. Her stomach did all sorts of turns and flips as she walked to the front of the class. She took a breath, reminded herself to talk more slowly, and thought back to all the advice she had gotten from her friends and the Bingham School children. She smiled to herself, staring out above everyone's heads, and described the process of baking prune *kolache*. She stumbled once, but recovered, and went on to give a recitation worthy of an A.

"You did it, Lena!" Emily beamed, as the girls filed out of the building later that afternoon. "See? Elocution isn't hard, after all."

"You were fantastic," Elenora agreed.

Milena let out a huge sigh of relief. "I'm just glad it's over," she admitted with a small smile. "Come on, we should get home so we'll be ready for the Forty Hours services tonight. And then the procession on Sunday."

"I'll see you both on Sunday, then," Emily grinned, waving them goodbye as Milena and Elenora headed west on Mayfield road toward their homes.

The closing service of Forty Hours at St. Gregory's turned out to be a beautiful affair. Milena, Elenora and many of their classmates marched in the procession. That afternoon there had been a brief but heavy thunderstorm, so instead of processing outside, they marched inside the church, around the pews. Each girl carried a candle, careful not to let the flickering flame go out, or to let any of the dripping wax burn their fingers. Father Riley followed behind them carrying the monstrance, while Jerry Sweeney, the altar boy, walked in front of the pastor, swinging a golden censer, filling the church with the sweet tang of incense. The flowery smoke tickled Milena's nose, but she managed to stifle her sneeze. At the end of the procession, the girls in their white dresses filed into the front pew, where they spent the next portion of the service in peaceful prayer before benediction.

Once the final hymns had been sung and the organ was silent, the congregation migrated downstairs into the basement social hall, beautifully decorated for the reception. Emily arrived a little late, and she could hear the music even before she stepped inside. Bohemian and Italian musicians filled the hall with melodies. When the wistful ballad "What'll I Do" began, Milena found herself swaying gently to the music. Hand in hand, young couples took to the dance floor. Milena sought out Elenora in the crowd, humming softly to herself.

She soon located the Morettis, gathered with other Italian neighbors on the right of the hall. Every so often a chorus of laughter would ripple through the group, loud enough to rival the musicians' tune. The Bohemians clustered in the opposite corner, the Doubeks among them. The German and Irish families were scattered around the hall, as Father Riley chatted with one family after the other, moving easily through the room. Words in several tongues mingled with the hum of English conversations.

Elenora and Milena drifted toward the table loaded with desserts. Elenora picked up three or four *cannoli*, and her lips were soon dusted white with powdered sugar. As Emily threaded her way toward them, she could hear Elenora telling Milena, yet again, how *her* mama was still the best cook in South Euclid. When she reached her friends, Elenora and Milena both grinned. "Emily! You're here at last," Elenora said, pulling her into a hug.

"Welcome to the party." Milena forced a brave smile. She glanced back at her family's corner, and even from across the room, she was able to catch some of Mr. Doubek's conversation. "I have been groundskeeper at the Rainbow several year now, and before with Novak," he was saying. "*Děkuji, děkuji.* Novak's garden, yes, lovely. I take pride." Milena tugged at the sleeves of her white sweater in irritation. She smoothed again and again the pleats of her white skirt, falling just below her knees, before she folded her arms across her chest. "Why does my family have to be so... *Bohemian* in public? I begged my mother to speak English."

"That's all right, Milena. I think it sounds pretty," Emily reassured her. "And this party is so much livelier than the socials we have at church. Methodists don't dance much," she said wistfully.

"Uh oh," Elenora whispered. "Look—Irena and Antonio are dancing. Together. In front of our parents." The musicians had started a polka. Irena and Antonio moved together in perfect step to the accordion's rhythms. Irena's pink dress, low-waisted with a subtly flaring skirt, swished around her knees as they danced.

"Papa!" It was Milena's younger brother Louis barreling past toward the Bohemians' circle, missing Emily by inches. The girls followed him with their eyes as he grabbed his father's hand, and tugged. "Papa, Papa!"

"*Promiňte, promiňte,*" Anton Doubek excused himself from the cluster of neighbors and frowned at his youngest son. "You know is rude to interrupt, Louis."

A devious grin tugged at Louis's lips. "But look, Papa, Irena's dancing with the Moretti boy!"

"What?" Anton straightened. He turned his eyes to the dance floor, locating his daughter, his face hardening. He strode towards the couple, Louis tagging behind.

Elenora let out an alarmed squeak and grabbed Milena's wrist. "Is he going to kill my brother?" she whispered.

"What you are doing, Irena?" Mr. Doubek said, loud enough to attract attention. Curious heads turned. Irena's feet stopped, but she did not drop Antonio's hand. Mr. Doubek said again, "*Co je to?*"

"'What is this?'" Irena repeated. "I'm dancing, Papa."

"Is this a problem, sir?" Antonio asked levelly. He locked eyes with Mr. Doubek, clutching Irena's hand.

Elenora's family had noticed the confrontation. Mr. Moretti reached the group in a few long strides, his wife not far behind. "With this one, Tony? We teach you better than this."

Mr. Doubek turned his attention to Antonio's father, his glare colder. "What you mean, 'with this one'? You not approve of my daughter?"

Elenora saw the stiffness of her father's jaw, the way he held his weight. His was not volcanic rage, but something more reserved, lurking behind his eyes. Mrs. Moretti placed a hand on his arm. The small gesture calmed him, slightly.

Mrs. Moretti glanced at Mrs. Doubek, cleared her throat, smiled, and turned to the pale girl at her son's side. "Irena, yes? Is a lovely dress. *Bella,* very beautiful." Irena mumbled her shy gratitude. Mrs. Moretti smiled, then, and glanced meekly at her husband.

Mr. Moretti frowned. Mr. Doubek mirrored him.

"And this music," Mrs. Moretti added. "It stirs the heart, no? See— my brother Tomaso is one of the accordion players."

"Our neighbor Svoboda play here, too," Mrs. Doubek said. "The music is good together, yes?" Slipping her arm into her husband's, she gave Mr. Doubek a stern glance.

Milena thought the silence would stretch into years. Then Mr. Moretti nodded, once. Mr. Doubek, with a small frown, conceded. "Good music, yes, need good dancing. Good dancers," he said quietly.

The tension dissipated, like a sigh through parted lips. Beaming, Antonio nodded respectfully to Mr. Doubek, then took Irena's hand and swept her back into the polka.

The two families slowly stepped back from the dancing couples, but instead of returning to their corners, they lingered in the middle of the hall. "Signora Doubek, you and your family, you come to our home next Sunday after Mass? For dinner? We live on Francis Court. Is not too far, *si?*" Mrs. Moretti asked.

Mrs. Doubek smiled. "No, is not far at all. Thank you, Paní Moretti. We are honored," she smiled, giving her husband's arm a squeeze.

"Maybe you bring *kolache* recipe for me? Your *dolci* very good," Mrs. Moretti said.

From their place near the desserts, the three friends shared surprised but happy glances. "I think I'm going to faint," Milena said. "You heard what they said? I'm not dreaming?"

Emily laughed, and Elenora elbowed Milena to assure her that she really wasn't dreaming. Milena brushed her away, but not before Elenora playfully nudged her again in the ribs, grinning. "You just wait and see. On Sunday, when you've tried some of my mama's pasta, you'll have to admit that she's the best cook in South Euclid."

The Heist and What Came of It:
A Story of South Euclid in 1935

The crisp November wind gusted through the windshield as Bill Ulrich drove his 1928 Model A down Mayfield Road. Even in 1942, the black hardtop coupe still ran great. His throat was a little dry; he was on his way to City Hall to be sworn in as a police officer for the City of South Euclid. As he approached Green Road in the early twilight, the lights of Hudson's Gas Station caught his eye. He and his

friend Dick Gerhardt had worked there when they were freshmen. The sight of the gas station brought to mind one of the most important days of his life, one that had first pointed him towards becoming a police officer.

As he braked for the light at Green, his eyes lingered on the gas station for another moment, and Mr. Schantz's grocery across the street. As he stared, memories came flooding back from 1935, when he was just fourteen.

· · · · · · · ·

The early November sky was overcast, with some sun peeking through the clouds. School had ended for the day, and Billy sat waiting on the steps of Brush High School with his best friend Dick Gerhardt, while students surged noisily around them. The red brick building loomed behind, the afternoon sun bouncing off the long rows of windows. Billy sat slumped over, holding the algebra test he had gotten back. A huge letter "C" was written in the corner in bright red ink. He shoved it into his pocket. "What's taking Charlie so long? He makes us wait every day, almost."

Dick looked at his friend for a second, crossing his arms before he responded. "Ever since Charlie's pop died he hasn't been in much of a hurry to get home. Can't blame him, though. I'd be pretty glum about it, too."

Billy frowned, but didn't say anything.

Charlie Rinaldi finally sauntered out of the school's doors a few minutes later. "Sorry about the wait, fellas. Mr. McDonough wanted to talk to me after class, since I failed that test," Charlie said, rolling his eyes.

"About time, Rinaldi! It's getting cold out here!" Billy said, pushing himself up from the stone steps. Charlie's grade made him feel better about his own C, but Billy still knew that his father would be furious. And he couldn't postpone seeing his father, because Mr. Hudson didn't need him today at the gas station. He tried his best not to think about it.

"Yeah, it is cold. I can feel that wind," Dick snickered, wiggling his fingers through the holes in his grey sweater. The three boys started walking, heading up the long driveway that curved toward Mayfield Road. Little clouds left their lips with every exhale.

Billy's stomach growled, loudly. "I could eat a cow, I'm so hungry. I haven't had a bite since lunchtime."

Dick scoffed at him. "At least you had a lunch today. Mom sent the last of the pot roast with my Dad this morning. He went back downtown looking for work."

"I think my mom's gonna have to water down the soup again tonight," Charlie said, wrinkling his nose. "Potato peels, onions and water: my *favorite*."

Charlie slowed his steps, stopping to pause at the Telling house. Billy and Dick slowed to a halt beside him. Charlie peered through the wrought-iron fence to look at the mansion. "Wouldn't it be nice to live in a house like that? No worries about the next time you are going to eat, and nice clothes with no holes in 'em."

A grin formed between Dick's ears. "Sounds like the life to me."

Charlie playfully punched Billy in the arm. "You know all about that good life, don't you, Mr. Butter and Egg Man?"

"Aw, you're all wet," Billy said. "My pop's a doctor, but we sure don't live in a mansion."

"I know, I know. We're just teasing ya, Egg Man," Dick said.

The boys continued their westward walk, leaving the Telling house behind them. Charlie shoved his hands in his pockets and was quiet for a while. He glanced at Billy, then at Dick, pondering. When he spoke again, his eyes were lit with mischief. "You know, I have a plan that could get some food into our moms' kitchens for a change."

"What you got cooking up in that brain of yours?" Dick asked.

Charlie draped his arms around his friends' shoulders as they walked. "Fellas, what if I told you that we have access to an unlimited food supply, and it's been sitting under our noses this entire time?"

Dick and Billy exchanged confused glances. "What're you talking about?" Billy asked.

"I work at Schantz's grocery store, remember? That store is loaded with food!" Charlie grinned confidently. "Mr. Schantz always takes his dinner at the same time every evening, early. When that happens, you guys come in. Dick, you can cause a distraction while I can take Billy down into the stockroom in the basement. The two of us could load up on all the cans we can carry, and then sneak out the back door! It's a perfect plan. Whaddya say?"

The boys were quiet for a long moment. Dick was the first to reply. "Sounds like we could pull this off. Count me in."

Billy's stomach churned. "But that's *stealing*. The cops could pinch us for that!"

"We won't get caught if we're smart about it. But listen, we don't have to go through with it. Just think about it, okay? Think about how much we could help our families." The boys had reached the corner of Mayfield and Green, when Charlie clapped Billy on the shoulder. "Well, I'm heading over to work. I'll see you guys tomorrow at school."

Dick waved. "See you, Charlie. Have fun on your day off, Billy. Abyssinia!"

Billy tried to smile back, but his mouth formed a grimace instead. "*Abyssinia* indeed. What a dumb thing to say," he grumbled to himself, turning north on Green at the bank, heading to his house on Lilac Road, while Dick stepped into Hudson's service station. He gave Dick a wave, but his head was a mess. When he reached his house, he shouldered open the side door, hung his jacket on the hook by the milk chute, and kicked off his shoes. The warm, sweet air of the house wrapped around him like a blanket, soothing the sting of the cold outside. Rob the grocery store? What was Charlie thinking?

Still lost in his thoughts, Billy pulled the algebra test from his back pocket, glanced at it for a second, and then crumpled it up. Trudging up the four steps into the kitchen, he tried to toss his math test basketball-style into the rubbish bin. He missed.

His little brother Arnie, in his usual hiding spot beneath the kitchen table, darted out and snatched the paper off the ground. "You stink!" he said. Arnie always got home from Victory Park School first, and would sometimes hide behind doors to try and scare Billy.

Mrs. Ulrich gently smiled at her eldest son from in front of the stove, where she stood stirring a pot of green beans. "Can you help set the table, Billy? Your father should be home any minute."

"Beans *again*?" Billy grumbled, but he went to the cabinets to grab the plates and silverware. He slipped into thoughts about the grocery store heist again, but jolted when he heard the front door open. His father was home. Billy ducked his head down, and hoped his father wouldn't ask about the algebra test. He had enough things to worry about.

Dr. Ulrich hung up his coat and hat and came into the kitchen. Draping her apron over a chair, Mrs. Ulrich smoothed out her polka-dotted house dress, and kissed his cheek. "Welcome home, Frank."

The family gathered around the kitchen table, where Mrs. Ulrich laid down a bowl of beans alongside a platter of mashed potatoes and what Billy considered to be a mighty scrawny-looking roasted chicken. Dr. and Mrs. Ulrich sat at the ends of the table, with the boys across from one another. After Mrs. Ulrich said grace, she dished out their dinner. Billy steered his beans across his plate with the tip of his fork, not really eating.

"How were the children today, honey?" Mrs. Ulrich asked, referring to the crippled children at Rainbow Hospital, where Billy's father worked.

"We operated on little Jane this morning. That hip. She came out of the anesthesia well, and she seems to be doing all right," Dr. Ulrich said.

Arnie swung his legs wildly under the table as he ate, striking Billy in the shin, and giggled into his plate. Not a minute later, he did it again. Billy gave him a scathing glare, resulting in more giggles.

"Mom," Billy whined, "Arnie's kicking me."

"Am not!" Arnie said pouting.

Mrs. Ulrich speared a piece of chicken with her fork. "Remember what Reverend Bischoff said during his sermon Sunday morning? We don't tell lies. Honesty is a virtue."

Billy slumped in his chair. He thought about the grocery store, which was a dishonest business indeed, and started to feel downright rotten.

"How was school today?" Dr. Ulrich asked him. "Did you find out how you did on that algebra test?"

"He sure did!" Arnie said before Billy could even respond. "He got a C and he crumpled it up and he tried to throw it away but I snatched it. I was gonna make it into a paper airplane but it was too wrinkly."

Dr. Ulrich's brow furrowed. "Is this true? A C on the algebra test?"

Billy stared down at his untouched food. "Yes, sir."

"I'm disappointed in you," Dr. Ulrich said with a shake of his head. "You're a smart boy. You could be doing much better. Maybe if you didn't waste so much time gallivanting around with those hoodlum friends of yours, you'd finally start to apply yourself."

It was Billy's turn to scowl. "Dick and Charlie aren't hoodlums! I'd rather spend time with them than spend all day studying for some lousy test."

"Your education is important. Don't you want to amount to anything when you grow up?" Dr. Ulrich asked.

"I sure don't want to grow up and work with sick kids all day, " Billy snapped.

Dr. Ulrich set down his fork, his voice a low growl. "You may leave the table."

"Fine!" Billy snarled. With a parting glare at Arnie for starting this whole mess, he shoved in his chair and stomped through the living room and up the stairs, slamming his heels into the floor, making his footfalls as loud as possible.

The nerve his father had, to say stuff like that! It was just a stupid math test; Dick and Charlie had nothing to do with it. They were his friends, and he was a louse to ever doubt them. In that moment, Billy decided to go in on the heist. He didn't care what his mom, or Pastor Bischoff, or anybody, especially his father, would think.

He would help them rob the grocery store.

The following Thursday, Billy and Dick were shivering outside Hudson's Gas Station, their canvas school satchels slung over their shoulders. Charlie had arranged for the boys to meet up at Schantz's Grocery Store at five thirty. According to Charlie, since the store closed at six, it would likely be empty of patrons and the boys would be able to pull off their heist without any witnesses. Billy and Dick just had to wait for Charlie to signal that the coast was clear.

Billy's teeth chattered as the wind tugged at his jacket. He could see Charlie in the store's brightly-lit window across the street, manning the cash register and talking to the grocer, Tom Schantz. A small-framed balding man, Mr. Schantz had always been kind to the neighborhood kids, passing out any leftover candies he had to clear when a new shipment came in. Now Billy could see him gesturing to Charlie, pointing to the back of the store, tapping his watch. Billy kicked at a bottle cap on the ground. He felt a little bad about stealing from this kind-hearted man, but Dick had assured him that Mr. Schantz would never know.

Billy looked up again and saw Charlie waving his hands at them. "That's the signal!" The boys hurried across Mayfield Road, slipping between the parked cars, and scrambled into the grocery store. Charlie held the door open for them, making a fist around the little bell attached to it so Mr. Schantz wouldn't hear it jingle. The odor of fresh paint and sealant still hung in the air, from when Mr. Schantz had tried to seal the cracks to block the November chill. Billy sniffled, his nose still red from the outside air. Three tight aisles packed with cans and bags made up the store. More cans were stacked in tin mountains on the ends of the aisles, with hand-drawn "Sale!" signs dangling from the ceiling with twine. No sign of Mr. Schantz.

"Okay, guys, the coast is clear," Charlie whispered, glancing over his shoulder. "Mr. Schantz is downstairs. He got a new shipment of canned goods in today, and he needs me down there to help him unload the crates and organize some stuff. Take what you want off the shelves up here. But you gotta be sure to get out of here before the cops come on their rounds for the night."

Billy's eyes widened to saucers. "Cops?"

Charlie waved his hand, brushing off his fears. "They don't come around till Mr. Schantz empties out the register. You know, they show up to make sure the money gets safe to the bank. Now, you guys got fifteen minutes—grab as much as you can and then head out the front."

Dick nodded in understanding. "Meet us behind Hudson's after you close. We'll divvy up the loot there."

Charlie grinned, flashing his teeth. "Grab me a box of Hostess," he said. He turned and quickly headed down one of the store's tight aisles, towards the back steps leading downstairs.

Billy and Dick shrugged off their satchels, opening them, and each headed down an aisle. Every shelf had cans and jars, boxes and bags nestled together. The colors and pictures on the labels blurred into a patchwork as Billy hurried to fill his bag. Sunblend's sloppy joe sauce, Cap canned meat, Mel-bro ham, and even exotic canned fruits like pineapples—he grabbed a couple of everything.

"Gee, look at all these canned hams! They should last us at least two Christmases," Dick chuckled, shoving a pair into his satchel.

Billy's mouth started watering as he turned down another aisle, where they kept the sweets: pastries from Hough and Laub, and Twinkies. Twinkies. Then he saw them.

"Cast an eyeball on these!" Billy said to Dick, holding up a box of Hostess cupcakes. "Mom never buys them 'cause she thinks they'll rot my teeth."

Satisfied with his pickings, Billy tried to close his bag. He had crammed it full to bursting with goods and couldn't get it shut. Some of the cans peeked out of the top.

The boys suddenly heard Charlie, a bit muffled, calling from the basement. "Wait, Mr. Schantz! You can't go up there yet. I think there's another crate down here!"

Billy's eyes widened in alarm. "We better scram." He started to hurry towards the front door, but skidded to a halt in the middle of the aisle. Through the front window, he saw two men in blue woolen uniforms crossing the street. The South Euclid policemen were early, and they were heading right for the store.

"Aw, applesauce!" whispered Dick.

"Quick, back door!" Billy said. He turned and bolted down the aisle, Dick at his heels. Billy's overstuffed bag knocked against the shelves. Something clattered, and Billy glanced back in time to see a couple of cans of Campbell's soup tumbling from a shelf. He wasn't looking where he was going, though, and ran smack into Mr. Schantz who was coming up the steps.

Billy fell backwards onto the floor, his satchel falling to the ground with a dull *thump!* The contents spilled out, the cans rolling wildly down the aisle. Dick was left standing behind Billy, clutching his own bag of would-be stolen goods tight against his chest.

As the boys stared up at the grocer in horror, Mr. Schantz, arms crossed, peered down at them. Billy thought he looked almost sad. "I come upstairs after a day of hard work to find empty shelves and a couple of thieves?" Mr. Schantz shook his head slowly. "You knew about this, didn't you, Charlie?"

Billy glanced past Mr. Schantz and spied his friend. Charlie stood stiller than stone on the second-to-last step, face paler than Billy had ever seen it. "Y-Yes, sir," Charlie croaked.

The bell on the front door jingled—a mockingly cheerful sound— as the two policemen finally walked into the store. Billy turned, and recognized the men as Officers Ford and Walsh.

"Is there a problem here, Tom?" Officer Walsh asked.

Mr. Schantz sighed, and nodded. "It seems like these boys thought they could make off with some of my stock."

Billy could feel his cheeks burn with shame. Officer Ford extended a hand, helping the boy to his feet. He then put one hand on Billy's shoulder, and the other on Dick's. Officer Walsh stepped forward to do the same to Charlie. "All right, boys. You better come with us to the station."

The officers led the three boys out of the store and across Mayfield, heading down toward the police station. It would be a long night for Billy and his friends.

- - - - - -

The traffic light turned green, snapping Bill's attention back to the present. Shifting gears, he made a right onto Green, heading toward City Hall, where the swearing-in ceremony would make him a police officer in his home town. His parents and his brother Arnie, Dick's folks, and Charlie's mom would be there, but not Charlie. Charlie was already at basic training in Rockford, Illinois. Charlie Rinaldi, private, United States Army.

Pulling into the City Hall parking lot, Bill turned off the ignition, got out and slammed the door. He stood for a minute with his hand on the still-warm hood, remembering that night when three very scared boys with empty canvas satchels had been brought to this very door.

The firm kindness of Officer Ford and Officer Walsh had made a difference.

Walking up the three stone steps to the double doors of City Hall, he turned toward the courtroom, just down the hall from the main entrance. In the hallway he was greeted by Mayor Oviatt. "Good afternoon, Mr. Ulrich. Are you ready for the ceremony?"

With a smile, standing upright and calm, Bill met Mayor Oviatt's gaze. "Yes, sir, I am."

The Mayor swung open the heavy maple door and led him into the courtroom. *Breathe, Billy. Take a deep breath and breathe. You have prepared for this moment. You have family and friends who are here to support you. You are ready.* He straightened the lapels of his blue wool jacket, checked his black belt to make sure the buckle was centered, and reached the brim of his hat to make sure it was straight. With long strides, Bill Ulrich entered the courtroom.

As he walked up the aisle, he saw from the corners of his eyes that the courtroom was full of family, neighbors and friends. Mayor Oviatt stood in front of the bench, with Chief Martin Schmies at the mayor's left. Bill placed his right hand on the Bible and announced confidently, "I, William Ulrich, do solemnly swear that I will support the Constitution of the United States and the Constitution of the State of Ohio, and that I will faithfully, honestly and impartially discharge the duties of a Patrol Officer for the Police Department for the City of South Euclid, Ohio, during my continuance in said office."

"Officer Ulrich," proclaimed Chief Schmies, "I am proud to name you a police officer of the City of South Euclid. Congratulations." As the Chief pinned the badge to Bill's uniform, people in the room stood up to applaud. Friends and family came forward to congratulate him.

"Billy, I am so proud of you," Mrs. Gerhardt said, with Mr. Gerhardt at her side. Bill could see his own parents smiling proudly. He was pretty sure his father's eyes were red.

Bill reached over to Mrs. Rinaldi, who wrapped her arms around him. "Charlie wrote from basic training, Billy, and says he's glad you're in uniform now, too." Her voice was small in the big room.

"How's he doing, Mrs. Rinaldi? How's the Army treating him?" Bill asked.

"Oh, he's doing well, Billy. It's hard, but he's brave. Like you. You're both in uniform, you two. We are so proud, so proud." Her voice trailed off, as she dug in her coat pocket for a handkerchief.

Dr. and Mrs. Ulrich stepped closer to their son. "Bill, your mother and I are proud," Dr. Ulrich said.

"Thank you, Dad. But before you say anything else," Bill said, "I've made plenty of dumb mistakes in my twenty-one years, but I hope you know I've put them behind me."

Dr. Ulrich put his hand on his son's shoulder and looked into his eyes, for what seemed an eternity. "You have, Bill. You're a man today."

Farewells and New Beginnings:
A Story of South Euclid in 1949

With the last word of *Kaddish* still hanging on the air, Rabbi Greenbaum reached out and removed the white sheet from the stone. The silken fabric slid away, smooth as water, exposing the newly placed grave marker and its inscription: *Benjamin Stein, 1925-1945.*

Joe Stein stood near the gravesite with his family for the unveiling ceremony, head bowed. His hand formed a fist around a small, smooth stone that he had been holding since the ceremony's start. This was little more than a memorial marker because his brother's body was far, far away from the little cemetery on Mayfield Road. Shadows of the surrounding trees fell across the stone's inscription, seeming to dance when the warm September wind touched the leaves. The air, heavy and hot and thick, clung to Joe like a second skin. Breathing was hard.

One by one, Joe's family moved forward to put pebbles on Ben's stone. It was a custom to leave the small stones to show that they had been there, honoring Ben. Joe's Grandma Rachel approached first, her grey braids pinned up around her head. Joe's father linked his arm in hers to support her frail frame. Joe's little sister Sarah went next, her dark braids hanging down her back. Then Joe's mother walked up. She stayed hunched near the stone for a long while, both her hands resting on the marble. When it was his turn, Joe stepped forward. Beads of sweat had collected on his forehead and cheeks like tears. He laid the tiny stone on the marker with a murmured prayer. The leaves rustled again, and Joe imagined the trees were whispering a prayer for Ben, too.

Ben had been killed in France, fighting the Germans during the War. It hurt Joe's mother to think that Ben might not have been given a proper Jewish burial, oceans away. It had pained her even more to have postponed the unveiling ceremony for so long. Ben had died more than four years ago. The Stein family had received word of his death from the War Department back then, but Grandma Rachel had refused to believe it. "Zey could have made a mistake," she would say. Her words were still flavored by the old country. "Vait to hold a service. You'll see. Benjamin vill prove them wrong. He'll come home." But he never did.

Then Mr. Stein found a new job at the Glenn L. Martin Company, and had moved the family from East 112th and St. Clair to South Euclid. When they were settled in their new house on Holmden, and Grandma Rachel had finally accepted Ben's death, they had planned the ceremony. The family had ordered the headstone from the Carabelli Company on Mayfield Road; Joe had gone with his father to pick out the marble and discuss the stone's design. The ceremony was bittersweet—Ben was gone and that hurt was still fresh, but Joe was relieved that his brother was finally being remembered.

"Thank you for doing this, Rabbi," Mr. Stein said, taking the rabbi's hand.

"It was a pleasure. Ben sounded like a fine man," he replied.

"He vas yust a boy, my Benjamin. Only nineteen years. He would have been someday a great man," Grandma Rachel whispered to no one in particular, "but the Master of the Universe had other plans."

Mrs. Stein looked back at the tree-shaded rows of stones, and dabbed at the corner of her eye with a handkerchief. "This is such a beautiful place. Ben would've liked it here, don't you think, Yosef?" Mrs. Stein said. She laid a comforting arm around her younger son's shoulders.

"He sure would've, Mom," Joe agreed.

The Stein family and Rabbi Greenbaum left the cemetery together, walking the short distance down Mayfield Road towards the bus stop on Coventry. The bus had been easier, Mr. Stein said, than to try to fit the whole family into his tiny Ford sedan. Sarah skipped over cracks in the bluestone sidewalk, but her step wasn't as springy as usual.

"So children, I hear you're both starting school on Tuesday," Rabbi Greenbaum said.

Joe squirmed, while Sarah gave him a bright nod. "We sure are, Rabbi. I'm going to Victory Park," she said.

"And you're going to Brush, aren't you, Yosef, not to the new junior high school?" Rabbi Greenbaum asked.

Joe nodded. Only seventh-graders were at the new school, and he was starting ninth grade. He had attended the new student orientation for freshmen just a couple of days ago. He'd toured the school, and sat in meetings where teachers explained a bunch of rules. It didn't help him feel better at all. He was missing his friends from the old neighborhood, and thinking about this new school left Joe's stomach feeling tight. The CTS bus approached, the doors squeaking open. Joe wrapped his fingers loosely around the metal railing as he trudged up the grooved stairs. Mr. Stein handed over a few dimes for everyone's fare, and the driver tipped his hat to Joe's father in acknowledgement. Then they all filed down the narrow aisle in search of seats.

By luck, Joe's parents found two empty seats together near the back. His grandmother plopped down near the front with Sarah, and Rabbi Greenbaum found his own seat somewhere in the middle. As Joe glanced around for an opening, a girl in a pink sundress caught his eye. A brown paper bag rested on her lap. She looked familiar, somehow. There weren't many open seats left, anyway, so Joe slipped in beside her. "Mind if I sit here?" he said.

"Go ahead," she shrugged. He thanked her, and the two of them quickly fell into a brief silence. She quirked her head, studying him, and suddenly smiled. "Hey, weren't you at the Brush orientation?"

"Yup," Joe nodded. "I thought I recognized you from somewhere."

She grinned. "I remember you. You stood out from everybody 'cuz of your little hat."

"You mean my yarmulke?" Joe reached a hand to touch the little circle of black fabric that always rested atop his head.

"Yeah, that. Sorry. I didn't know what it was called." She flashed him another smile. They came naturally to her, it seemed, like she was filled with inner sunshine. "I'm Lucrezia Spano. Nice to meet you."

"I'm Joe Stein," he said.

Lucrezia gestured to the bag on her lap. "Do you want some biscotti? My Nona Rosa made it. She always sends me home with tons of food."

Joe shook his head no, but he had to smile. His Grandma Rachel loved stuffing her grandkids, too.

Lucrezia shrugged. "Say, you didn't go to Victory Park last year for eighth grade, did you? I don't remember you."

Joe shook his head. "I used to go to school in Glenville, at Patrick Henry. My family moved here this summer."

"Oh, really? My friend Donny used to live in Glenville. I could introduce you to him, if you want," Lucrezia said. The two of them chatted for the rest of the ride. They discovered that they would have their first class together: Civics, with Mr. Hansen. Soon, though, the bus reached Warrensville Center Road, where the Steins would get off. While it was still rolling to a stop, Joe stood. But before he could step out into the aisle, Lucrezia stopped him.

"Would you want to meet up outside of Brush on Tuesday? We could walk to Civics together. I'm scared I won't be able to find the classroom," she admitted, biting her lip.

Joe grinned. "I sure would. Thanks. See you then, Lucrezia." Joe gave her a little wave, and hopped off the bus to rejoin his family. Now he had at least one friend in town.

On Tuesday morning, the day after Labor Day, Joe stood in the shadow of Brush High School, staring up at the building in awe. It loomed above him, one long wall with tall windows winking in the daylight. He had been there for orientation, sure, but the building still took his breath away. It seemed so much more elegant than his old school. A few students cast nosy, sidelong glances at Joe as they passed him. Most of the other kids just passed him by without a glance, their lighthearted laughter floating around him.

"*There* you are!" Lucrezia said, trotting up to Joe. Another boy, plump and short with a mop of sandy curls, stood beside her. "Joe, this is my friend Donny O'Connell. He's the one who used to live in Glenville when he was little," Lucrezia said.

Donny grinned at Joe, and they shook hands. "We lived on Brookwood, and I went to St. Aloysius for kindergarten and first grade. Then we moved out here. I know what it feels like to be the new kid. But don't worry, I can show you around town after school sometime. You play much baseball?"

Before he could answer, Joe found himself stumbling forward as one of the passing students rammed into his side. Joe barely caught himself, but his lunch bag tumbled to the ground. A group of girls walking nearby paused, their conversation halting, to watch the scene with wide eyes.

Joe straightened, and turned to face the kid who had shoved him. He was a lanky, scrappy-looking boy, with fiery hair and burning blue eyes. "Learn how to walk, jewboy," the kid sneered. Joe flinched at the word, his cheeks flushing. The group of girls quickly ducked their heads, and walked into the building with quickened steps.

"Don't you call him that, Patrick Treacy," Lucrezia snapped.

Pat frowned, half-turning to face her. "You're sticking up for the new kid, Lu? Don't you see that thing on his head?"

Donny folded his arms. "Go to class, Pat."

Pat snorted. "You guys have really flipped your lids." He shook his head and shoved his hands into his pockets as he swaggered up the steps.

Donny reached down and handed Joe his lunch. Lucrezia huffed a frustrated sigh. "Don't let it get to you, Joe. Pat grandstands all the time. He was a jerk at Victory Park, too."

"Thanks," Joe muttered, gripping the brown paper sack and reaching back to re-center his yarmulke. The sign of his faith seemed, now, like some big, bright, flashing target. Steeling himself, he stood straight, took a deep breath, and walked boldly into the building with Lucrezia and Donny—Pat Treacy or no Pat Treacy.

They headed down a couple of hallways lined with grey lockers. It was a madhouse, with students everywhere, fiddling with their lockers, clanging them shut, gossiping loudly to each other. Joe's ears thrummed.

It didn't take them long to find their first classroom: Civics. Maps of Ohio and the United States hung in front of the chalkboards all around the room. Mountains of textbooks stood on the window shelves and the back table, waiting to be distributed. A shiny pencil sharpener was attached to the wall nearest the door. Joe, Lucrezia, and Donny loitered in the back of the room with some of the other students, chatting, looking warily at the civics books. Mr. Hansen was already at the front of the room, printing the words *legislative, judicial* and *executive* on the board. Joe wrinkled his nose. How *boring*. Things got worse when, just as the bell rang, Pat Treacy sauntered in. Some other kids groaned at Pat's entrance, but Joe just tried to turn invisible.

Mr. Hansen, a kind-faced but stern-looking man, set down his chalk. "Welcome to Civics, and to ninth grade, my young citizens." His voice had gravel in it, that rough hoarseness that adults sometimes had when they weren't quite awake yet. Mr. Hansen picked up a clipboard, and adjusted his black-rimmed glasses. "I'm going to be giving you all assigned seats before we get started."

Starting with the seat near the front door and gesturing at each desk, Mr. Hansen read out names one by one. Joe tried to watch, wondering if he'd ever be able to match so many names and faces. When Mr. Hansen got toward the end of the alphabet, Joe started to pay closer attention. "Donald O'Connell. Karl Patterson. Margaret Ruberto. Lucrezia Spano. Yosef Stein. Mario Tamburro…"

Joe got placed in a seat in the middle of the row second from the windows. He slid into the desk, noticing that someone before him had carved a little heart into its wooden surface. Donny was a few seats ahead of him, but Lucrezia was right in front of him! Maybe they could pass notes to each other if the class got too boring.

"Patrick Treacy," Mr. Hansen called, and Pat stepped forward to take his place at the front of the next row. As he walked up the aisle of desks he swatted Joe in the back of his head with a quick *slap*, knocking the yarmulke to the floor.

"Whoops! I think ya dropped something," Pat snickered, adding (under his breath, so Mr. Hansen wouldn't hear), *"jewboy."* The students nearby heard the insult well enough, and the light chatter in the room fell to a quiet hush. Joe scrambled to reach his yarmulke, making a fist around it. His face hot, he sunk low into his seat, and considered crumpling it into a ball and shoving it into his pocket.

But before Mr. Hansen could say anything, Pat abruptly went flying, arms and legs flailing out as he fell to the floor face-first, letting out a startled squeak as his cheek hit the linoleum. The comic book he had been holding skidded toward Mr. Hansen, its pages flapping wildly. Joe looked up in time to see Donny quickly tuck his foot back underneath his desk. The class erupted into a chorus of laughter as Pat jumped to his feet and hastily scooped up his things. Pat's cheeks had grown almost as red as his hair. "Learn how to walk, Treacy," Rob Murphy muttered. Lucrezia turned slightly in her seat, caught Joe's eye, and smiled.

Mr. Hansen called for order, and the class instantly hushed. He scolded Pat and Rob for the disruption, then finished seating the rest of the students. Mr. Hansen launched into a lecture about the branches of government. Pat stared down at his desk, chewing on the end of his pencil for the rest of the hour. Joe put his yarmulke back on his head, and sat up straight as an arrow. He couldn't stop grinning.

Lucrezia and Joe didn't have any other classes together after Civics, but they found each other again in the cafeteria during the second lunch period. Grilled cheese was on the menu, and the warm smell of toasting bread filled every corner of crowded room. Joe and Lucrezia joined a table with Donny and Maggie. Rob joined them, too, once he got his tray from the lunch line, loaded with gooey grilled cheese, fruit salad, and a small bottle of milk.

"Did you see Pat's face in Civics today?" Maggie giggled. "His cheeks were redder than a tomato!" The cafeteria buzzed with conversation; Maggie had to shout a little so that the others could hear her.

"Are you kidding? His face was redder than Rob Murphy's when we dared him to eat that hot pepper in seventh grade," Donny chuckled, taking a big slug out of the bottle of milk on his lunch tray.

"My face wasn't *that* red," Rob said.

Joe unpacked his lunch—a kosher meal from his mom—as they spoke. Lucrezia had a packed lunch, too. She pulled out an apple, some biscotti, and a prosciutto sandwich, and systematically began pinching off its crust. "Are you and your families going to the dedication on Sunday?" she asked.

"Dedication?" Joe frowned. "What dedication?"

"The city's re-dedicating the War Memorial monument on Sunday afternoon," Lucrezia replied. "My brother Vince helped Mr. Robertino with the stonework. Vince fought in the war, too. He has a scar to prove it." Lucrezia was quiet for a moment. She set down her sandwich. "The monument's going to have all the names of South Euclid men killed overseas. My... my dad's name is going to be on it."

"I'm so sorry," Joe said softly. "My brother Ben was killed during the war, too. I know how that feels."

Lucrezia smiled at him, gratefully. "You and your family should come. It's at Victory Park. Two o'clock."

When his family stepped off the CTS bus and looked across the street at Victory Park School, Joe couldn't believe how many people were gathered for the dedication. It seemed like the whole town of South Euclid was there. On the grass on either side of the school's front walk, the school janitors had set up rows of folding chairs, most of which were already filled. A podium had been set up facing the school. Mayor Urban stood near it, with some clergymen, and several other men, probably the councilmen. Joe heard his father whisper to his mother, pointing out Governor Lausche among the dignitaries.

It was a warm day, almost too warm for the middle of September, even warmer than last Sunday when the Stein family had held the unveiling ceremony for Ben. Joe spotted Lucrezia and her family in one of the back rows, farthest from Mayfield. Joe nudged his mother and father, and together they wove their way through the milling crowd.

Part way toward the school building, Joe stopped cold. Patrick Treacy was sitting two rows in front of Lucrezia. He would have to walk by Pat Treacy to get to the Spanos. Joe noticed that Pat was sitting with a woman in a powder-blue dress, undoubtedly his mother—her hair and Pat's were the same bright red—and three younger children, all red-haired, and all sitting very quietly. Mrs. Treacy was blowing her nose quietly into an embroidered handkerchief. Just then Pat looked up, and his eyes met Joe's. The two boys stared at each other in silence for a moment. Joe hesitated, unsure whether to continue towards Lucrezia's family and risk more of Pat's wrath. He couldn't handle another blow from Pat when his heart was heavy with thoughts of Ben.

To his surprise, though, Pat's eyes didn't have the fire in them that he had seen all week at school. They were softer. Pat gave a small nod. "Hey, Joe," he whispered, standing next to his chair.

Joe stretched out his hand. "Hi, Pat."

Pat took Joe's hand, nodded, sat down again, and put his arm around his mother's shoulder. Then Joe realized that Pat must be here for the same reason he and Lucrezia were. His dad's name must be on that memorial too.

With his parents just behind him, Joe led the way past the Treacys toward the last rows of chairs, very close to the school's front doors. Lucrezia and her brother stood as Joe and his family approached. "Mom, Dad, this is Lucrezia Spano." He took a breath, and hesitated, and said again, "This is my friend Lucrezia. And this is her mom, and her brother Vince."

Mr. Stein greeted Mrs. Spano, and extended his hand to Vince warmly. "Joe tells me you fought in Holland. It's good to meet you."

"Thank you, sir. It's a pleasure to meet you, too," Vince smiled. Joe could pick out the thin white scar that ran through Vince's left eyebrow and down toward his ear. Joe slipped over to Lucrezia's side, sitting next to her as Mrs. Stein and Mrs. Spano began to chat.

People took their seats and a relative hush fell as the clergymen gathered near the podium for the benediction. Then Mayor Urban began his remarks. "Welcome, fellow citizens, and thank you for coming. We are gathered here today to show our gratitude for the ultimate sacrifice made by these twenty-three sons of South Euclid during that terrible war…" Joe tried his best to listen, but he kept getting lost in memories of Ben. Mrs. Stein tugged out her handkerchief again. Joe saw Mrs. Spano lean over to lay her hand on Mrs. Stein's wrist.

The Governor talked for a little bit, and then the Methodist pastor, Reverend Lamb, was introduced. He described how South Euclid had pulled together during the War, buying war bonds, writing letters, supporting the Gold Star families, and about how proud everyone was of these young men.

Joe glanced over at his friend. Lucrezia's jaw was set, and her eyes shone like glass, but no tears had fallen. Joe nudged her. "You okay?" he whispered.

"I'm fine." She glanced at him, flashing him a brave quick smile before turning away again.

"They were our sons and brothers, our fathers and neighbors," Reverend Lamb was saying. "We are proud to call these men heroes. Because of this memorial, we will never forget their sacrifice and selflessness."

"It's true, you know," Joe whispered again. "Your dad and Vince and Ben and even Pat's dad—they all did something great."

Lucrezia smiled at him again, one of her sunny ones this time. "Thanks, Joe. I'm really glad you're here."

Finding Her Own Way:
A Story of South Euclid in 1956

"I'm going to find a way!" Caroline LaMarca said. She flashed her friend a determined little grin, and took a big bite of pizza.

Everybody who was anybody knew that the best place to go after school was Geraci's. The little pizza shop on Cedar at Green had just opened in July, and once the school year had started many of the Regina girls made it a point to stop for a slice of pizza on their way home. Besides, sitting in the restaurant's warm, delicious air was much more appealing than waiting in the biting December wind for the #32 bus.

Kathy Stevic, Caroline's self-appointed best friend, frowned at her from across the table. Sighing, Kathy tucked a flyaway strand of black hair back behind her ears. Her ever-present babushka was around her neck now, ready to be pulled up again when she had to face the outdoors. Kathy always wore a babushka, and had a whole rainbow of them to suit her moods. Today's fabric was green with white polka dots. "I don't know, Caroline. Maybe you should just wait until next year," Kathy said.

Caroline huffed, sinking back into her chair. Absently, she breathed in the aroma of sweet tomatoes, bread and garlic that hung thick in Geraci's and tried to think of a comeback. A chorus of giggles from the back corner of the restaurant caused Caroline's head to turn. It was her older sister, Marianne, laughing with a group of her friends. A senior, Marianne was already looking forward to graduation, and making her plans to enter the convent. Today, though, Caroline could hear Marianne and her friends talking about the auditions for Regina's spring play, *Queen Esther*.

Caroline watched as Kathy bit into her pepperoni pizza. The cheese clung to the pizza in long, waggling strings. She had been hungry earlier, but Kathy's discouraging attitude had quickly made her lose her appetite. "I don't want to wait. Notre Dame College might not have a whole afternoon of science demonstrations next year. This could be my only chance to see what careers are out there for me." She made a determined fist in her lap. "I'm going to the one on Friday."

"Our Christmas concert is Friday," Kathy reminded her. "It counts for our final grade in Glee Club. Sister Joanmarie will fail you if you skip it."

Caroline made a face. She already had a B- in Glee Club, but she just couldn't force herself to focus on melodies when she could be focusing on mitochondria. She knew that most of her classmates had other aspirations. If Marianne went to the convent, she'd be a teacher. Kathy was beginning to think about being a teacher too. So when Sister Mary Meta, her biology teacher, had told Caroline that the science students at NDC would be giving a whole slew of presentations and demonstrations this Friday afternoon, she knew she had to go. She just had to. "This is about my future, Kathy," she sighed.

"Oh, not this again. You sure have a big mouth when something's on your mind, Carrie," Marianne said, coming to stand by Caroline's table. "It's like I told you yesterday. You can't skip the concert—especially since we're combining with the Notre Dame Academy choir. And you don't want to abandon the alto section, do you?"

Caroline had to admit that, no, she didn't. Some of the altos, particularly that Virginia Pulnik, were absolutely dreadful. Caroline suspected that Virginia might be tone deaf. "But NDC is right across the field. It's so close to Regina—it's the opportunity of a lifetime," Caroline begged.

Marianne sighed (rather melodramatically, Caroline thought). "Come on, Carrie. Let's get to the bus stop. We have chores to finish up before dinner, you know."

"In a minute. Let me finish my pizza," Caroline said. A tiny, little seed of an idea had entered her head.

Marianne shrugged. Clutching her armload of books, she headed towards Geraci's front door. As the door closed behind her, Caroline turned to Kathy. "I won't have to abandon the alto section. I could go to the concert and NDC! See, the science program starts at four o'clock," she explained. "The concert doesn't start until seven-thirty. I can go over to Notre Dame for some of the presentations, and then head back to Regina right before the concert starts. It's perfect!"

Kathy shook her head. "The NDA choir is coming to Regina at four for a mandatory rehearsal, remember? It's our only one with them before the concert. Then at five-thirty Sister Eymard is serving us all dinner. I think she's making tuna fish sandwiches—although everybody knows your mom makes the best tuna salad in the world." Caroline had to smile at that. "But anyway, after dinner we get our corsages, warm up, get in line, and at seven-thirty we take the stage,"

Kathy said, rattling off the schedule from memory. She had written a story promoting the concert for *The Regent*. It had made the front page.

Caroline furrowed her brows, thinking. "What if I—"

"Carrie!" Marianne called, from Geraci's doorway. "Hurry up, the bus is almost here."

Caroline stood from the table. She scooped up her schoolbooks from the table, cradling them in her arms as Kathy snagged Caroline's untouched slice of pizza. The concert wasn't until Friday. "I will find a way," Caroline said again, and ran out of Geraci's to join her sister.

* * *

The rest of the week dragged on for Caroline. The long walk that she and Marianne made when it wasn't too snowy, from their house on Wrenford, down Bayard, across Belvoir, up Greenway and then finally to school, seemed to last hours.  Every day when she walked through the white doors near the flagpole, stomping snow off her saddle shoes, she would try once again to come up with some sort of plan, but every morning she fell short.

Distracted, Caroline fumbled through her classes. Sister Mary Lynn's Latin conjugations quiz was a total disaster on Monday. For Tuesday's Advent chapel visit, she nearly forgot to put on her chapel cap. If Kathy hadn't reminded her to grab the little piece of black velvet from her locker, boy, it would have been bad. The only class she thrived in was biology with Sister Meta. Her homeroom was the biology lab, 213, with its long black-topped lab tables instead of desks. Caroline loved it. The side wall had six large windows that the sun poured through in the mornings. While her lab partner was busy drawing squiggles in eraser on the tabletop, Caroline was charting genetic trait grids faster than anyone else in the class.

Thursday was the worst day of all—maybe the worst day of her life. Her mind was so preoccupied that when she was heading for the choir room, she almost got smacked in the face when one of the Student Council officers walked out of the double doors as she was going in. To make matters worse, she sounded dreadful; her voice cracked on all the high notes in "O Holy Night." Even Virginia Pulnik sounded better than she did. How embarrassing! Caroline spent her lunch period that day crying in the kitchen. There was a tall wooden stool at the end of Sister Eymard's long counter, near the walk-in cooler and the back door. Many heartbroken girls sat on that stool and wept. Sister understood that, sometimes, all a girl needs is a good cry.

At the end of the lunch period, Caroline was feeling much, much better. In the kitchen she saw that white back door to the parking lot, next to the delivery entrance. Now, she had a plan. She had more than a plan: she had an escape route! Notre Dame College, here I come! she thought as she skipped up the stairs to geometry.

Finally, Friday arrived. It was, without a doubt, the slowest school day of Caroline's life. When eighth period was over, she bolted from her desk to meet up with Kathy in the cafeteria. Caroline flew down the south stairs, and headed through the cafeteria hall, sparing a brief glance at the bulletin board, littered with dittoed flyers advertising the *Queen Esther* auditions, and the post-Christmas intramural basketball tournament. A sharp, fishy smell was already creeping out from the kitchen across the hall. Sister Eymard must be starting the preparations for dinner already. Caroline pushed through the doorway into the cafeteria. Most of the Glee Club was already here, clustering around textbooks and notebooks, doing some homework as they waited for the NDA bus to arrive. Caroline quickly spotted Kathy, and threaded her way through to her table. She sat down and whispered, "I'm skipping rehearsal today to go to NDC, and I need your help. And before you say anything, I'll be back before the concert starts. I promise."

Kathy narrowed her eyes, not convinced. "But Caroline…"

"I'm going to sneak out through the kitchen, through that back door. I'll just cut across the parking lot and then the field, and I'll be at NDC in no time. I just need you to promise to cover for me if Sister Joanmarie gets suspicious," Caroline said. "Please, Kath?"

Kathy's face held expressionless for a few moments, but finally a devious grin appeared. "We're best friends. Of course, I'll help," she said.

It wasn't long before the bus from Notre Dame Academy arrived. The girls flooded into the cafeteria, laughing and chattering as they looked around Regina with wide, curious eyes. The NDA girls were a sea of white blouses, navy jumpers and saddle shoes. The chatter in the cafeteria soon grew to a laughing roar. "Now's your chance," Kathy said, and pointed across the room. Caroline glanced up and saw Sister Joanmarie at the other end of the cafeteria, flipping through sheet music with a senior named Barbara, one of Marianne's friends, who accompanied the Glee Club on piano, and another Sister that Caroline guessed was the Notre Dame choir director. Caroline grinned at Kathy and scooped up her textbooks—she couldn't very well leave them in the cafeteria, after all—glanced back once, then slipped into the empty hall. No going back now.

Caroline slid between the silver steam tables, where the Sisters dished out the hot lunch. She stood on tiptoe outside the swinging doors leading into the kitchen, peering through one of the two round windows that always made Caroline think of owl eyes. She saw a platter half-full of tuna sandwiches, the stoves, the beige tile walls, but no Sister

Eymard. The coast was clear! She pushed open one door and slipped in, heading for the back door.

A voice stopped her. "Caroline LaMarca? What are you doing back here?"

Caroline's legs locked at the sound of Sister Eymard's warm voice, and her books slipped from her arms, hitting the floor with a loud slap! Sister Eymard had just stepped out of the walk-in cooler with a huge jar of pickle relish in her hands. Caroline's cheeks flushed as she fumbled for an excuse. "I… was just…"

Much to her surprise, Sister Eymard chuckled. Setting the relish on the counter, she bent down and scooped up Caroline's books. "I had a hunch you might be here, ever since that tearful episode yesterday," she said. Sister Eymard moved down the counter, where one tray of tuna sandwiches was ready, and a big bowl of tuna and mayonnaise waited to be mixed. Sister scooped some relish in and began mixing. "Just leave your books on that windowsill, honey. I'll make sure no one fusses with them until you get back."

Caroline did so, turning to set her books on the beige tile ledge. "Thank you, Sister."

"Here. I expect you won't be back in time for supper." Sister Eymard smiled, handing her one of the tuna sandwiches already wrapped in wax paper. "I never much cared for choir rehearsals, either. If you're not ready the day of the concert, flapping your jaws ten minutes before won't do anyone much good," Sister Eymard winked.

With a grateful smile, Caroline slipped out through the kitchen door to the parking lot. Fat grey clouds loomed overhead. She took a deep breath, filling her lungs with the wintery air, crisp with the promise of snow. She sprinted across the parking lot towards the grass, heading across the field near the tennis courts instead of taking the sidewalk past the faculty house to Lawnway. Everybody knows a diagonal path is shorter than a right angle! She headed toward the Gothic spire of Notre Dame's building, around the grassy circle to the doorway that seemed hidden in the shadow of the tall chapel wing. Looking back at Regina, she felt her stomach do a flip-flop. Caroline felt a little guilty for sneaking around and having Kathy lie for her, but she decided that being a liar and a coward was worse than being just a plain old sneak. Putting on her bravest face, she headed into the College.

***

Meanwhile, Kathy was playing tour guide. Nancy and Donna, two of the NDA girls that she knew from grade school at St. Ann's, had practically begged her to show them around the still-new Regina High. Kathy took them up the south staircase to the second floor, and the trio roamed the halls with a couple of sandwiches Kathy had snuck out of the kitchen.

"These are fantastic," Donna said, with a big bite still in her mouth.

"Sister Eymard is a great cook," Kathy agreed, "but everybody knows Caroline LaMarca's mom makes the best tuna salad sandwiches in the world. They're practically legendary."

Nancy poked her head into the middle classroom: 211 Chemistry. "I still can't believe you don't have to wear uniforms! You're so lucky," Nancy said, tugging on the neckline of her blue jumper with a disgruntled look.

"These things are just plain awful."

"I think they're kind of cute," Kathy admitted. "We do have gym uniforms. You should see those things! Everyone hates them. They're like green potato sacks!"

The girls laughed, and Kathy led them down the north steps and into the hall to the choir room. The girls had great fun comparing everything from wall paint to choir warmup routines. Eventually, they finished their sandwiches and made their way back downstairs to the cafeteria for rehearsal. Under Sister Joanmarie's instruction, the girls had pushed some of the tables and chairs out of the way for the rehearsal. Sister wanted enough space for them to run through a few of the songs in their proper order, so there would be no surprises once they took the stage.

"When do we get our corsages?" Donna asked.

"I think they're handing them out to us after dinner. Nobody wants to sing with pickles among your holly berries!" Kathy giggled. Sister Joanmarie arranged the choir, mixing Regina and NDA. But as she looked over the choir, Sister Joanmarie's brow furrowed. Kathy cringed.

Her blue eyes narrowing, Sister Joanmarie asked, "Where's Caroline?"

***

 Caroline bolted out of Notre Dame's chemistry lab and dashed for the outside door. Stupid, stupid, stupid! she scolded herself. She had been so engrossed in the chemistry presentations that she had completely lost track of time. What was the schedule again? Were they lining up at seven-fifteen? Were they still in warm-up? Were they heading onstage? Please, Lord, don't let me be late! Caroline sprinted back across the field. Snow fell in fat flakes, clinging to the fabric of her jacket and catching in her eyes. Caroline sprinted the distance between buildings in under a minute.

She rushed back into the back door of the kitchen, breathless. Wiping down the center counter, Sister Eymard looked up as she burst in.

"Am I late? Did they go onstage already?" Caroline huffed. She didn't bother reclaiming her books from the windowsill; she would do that after the concert. If she made it to the concert!

"You're just in time. They're getting lined up now," Sister Eymard said, nodding toward the hallway. Caroline thanked her, and slipped out through the far door into the crowded corridor. The combined choirs were a whispering blur of long-sleeved white blouses with corsages of red carnations and holly sprigs tied with white ribbon at their left shoulders. Frantically, Caroline wound her way to the middle of the line where the altos stood, only half-heartedly trying to stifle their pre-concert giggles. Sister Joanmarie was at the far end of the hall, gesturing for quiet. She caught Caroline's eye, and the latter, blushing guiltily, wedged herself into line between Kathy and Nancy. Marianne was with the sopranos in the front of the line. Caroline was pretty sure her sister too had seen her wander in. She winced at the thought.

"There you are, Carrie," Kathy hissed. "I had to tell Sister Joanmarie you went to the bathroom. Twice. And I don't think she believed me the first time."

"You're a pal," Caroline wheezed.

"Here. I grabbed this for you," Kathy said, giving Caroline the extra corsage that she had been clutching. Caroline thanked her profusely as Kathy pinned it on, and then ran her fingers through her pixie cut, hoping the melted snow wouldn't totally flatten her bangs. The whispers diminished, and Sister Joanmarie led them down the hall, past the stairs and into the locker rooms.

"So?" Kathy whispered, nudging her friend. "Was it good?"

Caroline's eyes lit up. "It was wonderful! One of the College girls taught me to solve chemical equations, and another girl was talking to me about becoming a research scientist, and the College is so pretty!"

Single-file, the girls walked past the lockers and showers, into the scenery storage room, and then clattered up the four wooden steps onto the risers behind the green velvet curtain. Caroline loved this part, right before the show, the tense silence of the choir opposite the thrum of the audience's conversations.

Then all at once the curtain was pulled back, to the welcome sound of applause. Caroline quickly spotted her parents in the second row of beige metal folding chairs set up for the occasion. She marveled at how the gym was transformed for concerts—black curtains drawn across the high side windows and the three windows above the bleachers. It made the gym seem even warmer on the crisp December evening.

Behind a music stand on a small wooden platform behind the last row of metal chairs, Sister Joanmarie was just a vague black outline in the dim light, but when she raised her white-gloved hands, Caroline had no problem seeing her. All the girls straightened. Sister Joanmarie gave the cue, and the altos hit the starting *thum, pum pum's* of "The Little Drummer Boy."

It was a fantastic concert. The two choirs' voices blended in a rich, layered sound, as if they had been singing together their whole lives. Even Virginia Pulnik was on key. Caroline knew that, after the concert was over, she'd have to tell Marianne, her parents, and Sister Joanmarie the truth. She and Kathy both would probably get a scolding, but in that moment, she didn't care. Smiling a little, Caroline gave herself to the harmonious sound around her. That harmony was inside, too, now, and she was pleased.

Outsiders, Insiders, and a Few Simple Gifts:
A Story of South Euclid in 1975

As Muriel Young stirred some warm cereal for little Leslie, who was happily patting the tray of her highchair, she was watching her three older children eating breakfast. Keith, a fourth-grader, and Judy, a first-grader, were chattering about the cider and donuts treat that the Lowden PTA was having at school this afternoon. Her eighth-grader Greg was silent, toying with the AlphaBits in his bowl. The move from Detroit to South Euclid had been the hardest on him, Muriel thought. She and her husband had hoped that Greg's interests in band and wrestling might help him make the transition, but while he had once had a few close friends, he now seemed adrift. She and Don had met only three other Afro-American couples at the junior high orientation night for new families. She was sure that being one of only a few black children at Memorial was taking a toll on Greg.

Muriel gathered her courage as she sat down to feed Leslie. "How's band, Greg? Have you started on Christmas music yet?" she asked, as brightly as she could.

"Not much, Mom," Greg replied, still studying his cereal bowl. "We're working on some Aaron Copland and George Gershwin for the bicentennial show in the spring."

"Your dad would love to hear you on the Gershwin," Muriel offered.

"I wish he'd be home so I could play it for him," Greg whispered. The truth was, playing the saxophone was starting to exhaust him. It had been something that he did to make his dad proud, but his dad was on the road so much that they rarely saw him anymore.

"I know how you feel," Muriel replied. "Once he's learned the regional sales markets for East Jordan, he'll be home more." Judy and Keith were listening now, wide-eyed and a little sad. "This weekend he'll be back from Columbus, and we'll do something together," she smiled.

Twenty minutes later, having dropped off the little ones at Lowden Elementary, Mrs. Young turned the station wagon south on Green Road, heading toward Memorial. They passed the East Jordan Iron Works, the cement factory, and the same houses, block after block. Greg really missed shooting the breeze with his dad.

"What's new in school this week, Greg?" Muriel inquired gently.

"Not much," he replied. "Just the usual, uninteresting, a little bit of torture."

"Do you think you might try out for wrestling, honey? I know you didn't like it much back home," Mrs. Young said, turning left on Liberty.

"Probably not," Greg said, staring out the window as the trees and houses slipped past. "Band and school are enough. And getting to know kids." He felt a sudden wash of cold loneliness.

As they pulled into the parking lot next to the glass-and-brick school, Greg noticed Debbie Zaccaro getting off the school bus. She sat behind him in English and math. She was one person who actually knew  his name. Maybe he could catch up to her.

"Thanks, Mom," Greg said, leaning over to give her a quick kiss.

"What time should I pick you up? Is there wrestling tonight?" Mrs. Young asked hopefully.

"No, Mom, just the regular time. See you!" Greg slammed the car door and rushed for the main doors. Mr. Cirillo greeted him, but Greg just waved and drove straight for homeroom, even though he was fifteen minutes early. From the doorway, he saw that Debbie Zaccaro was already at her desk. Maybe they could talk a little before announcements. But then he saw that ninth-grader sitting opposite Debbie, that wrestler Steve. The reason Greg wasn't going out for wrestling.

It wasn't till second period English that Greg felt brave enough to talk to Debbie. All around the room students were dragging their desks into groups of five. Greg wiped his sweaty palms on his plaid bell-bottoms, sat back down, and opened his battered copy of The Outsiders. This was his third time reading it, but it never got old. This year he loved it more than ever. Mrs. Harvan was distributing dittoed questions they had to talk about in groups. Glancing around, it seemed that most of his classmates were more concerned with their bubble gum and carving rude insults into the well-worn desks.

Greg shook his head. He couldn't understand these South Euclid kids. Everyone he had hung out with back in Detroit liked reading. How did these kids not get it? Books were just as good as anything on television (except maybe <u>Starsky and Hutch</u>), yet everyone seemed completely uninterested. Then Debbie started talking. Again.

"Okay, here are the questions," she said, methodically passing out the still-cold purple-printed sheets. Greg thought they smelled like rubbing alcohol. "Take a minute to look them over." This girl sounded like the teacher. Good grief!

These questions had such easy answers: *Why is Ponyboy considered an outsider? Who is represented more positively, the Greasers or the Socs?* It was all so obvious, but one question surprised him: *Is Cherry an outsider?*

"Cherry's the best character. Of course she's not an outsider," Debbie chirped.

"You only like her because she's about the only girl in the book," Scott taunted. Debbie's eyes clouded and her cheeks flushed.

Greg was confused. Didn't Debbie see the risks Cherry was taking being seen with Ponyboy and Johnny? "The Socs and the Greasers are equals," Greg blurted. "They're both gangs, and both are dangerous. The only difference is that one gang's got more money than the other." Greg was surprised he felt so strongly.

Scott, Pam, Cheryl and Debbie all turned to look at him. Scott shook his head. "Whatever. This book is stupid," he said dismissively.

The five of them remained quiet for a long time, with the hum of discussion all around them. Scott was coloring in all the *o*'s and *e*'s and *a*'s on the handout. Cheryl and Pam were giggling about something. Debbie was paging through chapter two.

Then Debbie spoke up. "You know, I think you're right. At the drive-in, here, Cherry seems really nervous talking with Ponyboy." She was sitting a little straighter, her eyes searching the ceiling for what she really wanted to say. "Kind of embarrassed about being a rich kid."

Greg pointed to the first page of chapter three. "Here's Ponyboy talking: 'It seemed funny to me that Socs—if these girls were any example—were just like us.' That's what the book is getting at, to me." Greg felt out of breath. He hadn't said that much in a class in the whole six weeks he'd been at Memorial.

"So Cherry figures out that Ponyboy is, you know, a real person," Debbie said quietly, giving Greg a long look.

Greg heard a gentleness in her voice, and he knew exactly why. Till this very minute, he had felt like an outsider all the time in South Euclid, whether he was at Mancuso's with his mom shopping for groceries, or in school watching all the cliques. As much as he liked to pretend it didn't bother him, he knew deep down the only place he belonged wasn't here. But maybe Debbie was getting it, too: what it felt like to be an outsider.

* * * * *

By the end of third period band, when the strains of the "Simple Gifts" segment of <u>Appalachian Spring</u> faded, Greg rested his saxophone on his knees and listened as Miss Burgess offered some praise for how quickly they were learning the piece, and some segments that each instrument should work on before tomorrow's class. Greg liked this Copland work. It made him look forward to the Bicentennial concert next spring.

"This is better than 'Frosty the Snowman' in October, don't you think?"

The boy in front of him, the saxophone section leader, was grinning up at Greg, who was desperately racking his brain for the guy's name. So he made a project of sliding his music back into his folder. "Yeah, I guess," he replied.

"You're pretty good at the sax, man!" said the section leader. "My name's Tim Cassidy. I live on Delevan, off Richmond, over near the Mall. You going to lunch now?"

"Y-yeah, I am. I'm Greg Young. I live on Princeton, the other side of Belvoir."

"You just move here?" Tim asked casually, but with a smile that said he was really interested.

"Yeah. My dad works for East Jordan Iron Works, and he got transferred here this summer. So we moved." That sounded so dumb. Greg wished he could disappear under the linoleum.

Miss Burgess was already turning off the band room lights, so Greg and Tim walked together to the instrument storage units in the hall. Greg had hoped to escape to lunch unnoticed, but it seemed like Tim was gluing himself to Greg. Maybe this would be okay.

"Well, let's grab some grub, man," Tim grinned, clasping the padlock shut on his locker. At that moment, the unfamiliar face became familiar. This could be better than okay.

The two elbowed their way through the crowded corridor and into the even noisier cafeteria, still talking as they stood in the lunch line. Tim listened while Greg told about his old school near Detroit, and Greg heard about Tim's band career, his experience as a Memorial Mustang wrestler, and his Saturday afternoons cruising Richmond Mall. They talked all the way through the line and over to the table where Tim sat with his ninth grade buddies. Greg stood frozen. The kid on Tim's left was the same guy that had knocked Greg's books out of his hands a couple of weeks ago. The same guy who hung out with Debbie all the time. The same guy that ragged on him for being "that dumb new kid." Or for being "that colored kid."

"Sit down, Greg. I want you to meet the guys," Tim smiled, pulling out a chair for him. "Greg, this is Steve, and Tony, and Kevin, and Mike, and Angelo. Guys, this is Greg. He's a darn good saxophone player, I want you to know."

Greg nodded quietly to the ninth graders, mumbling "hey" to each one.

"Steve, I was just telling Greg how neat it would be if he came out for wrestling," Tim chattered on. "Don't you think Greg should try out?"

The abrupt silence at the table seemed to echo through the cafeteria. Steve looked Greg up and down, and then leaned over and whispered in Tim's ear. Tim flushed, and gave Steve what seemed to Greg a pretty angry look. Suddenly Tim stood up. "Hey, Greg, it's nice outside. Let's go out there and eat." His mouth a tight line, Tim grabbed his tray and headed for the outdoor courtyard. Greg followed, puzzled.

"What was that all about?" Greg asked as they settled in at a picnic table. "Oh, wait. I know." Greg paused. "Steve doesn't mix with colored, right?"

"Don't worry about it, man. Steve is just a chump. Now c'mon, let's eat."

Lunch that day was the best Greg had had at Memorial, and not because of the brownie. He felt good having lunch with a ninth-grader, a guy with friends. Greg thought there might be half a dozen Afro-American students in the building, mostly girls, but none in any of his classes. An eighth-grader named Tyrone had a locker near Greg's, but he had fifth period lunch. He hadn't yet found any Afro-American friends, but Greg was pleased to find a friend in Tim.

As they carried their trays back in to the cafeteria, Tim elbowed Greg, pointing to a yellow flyer taped to the wall. "See—that's the thing about wrestling tryouts this Friday."

"Yeah? After what Steve said, I think I'll stick to my saxophone," Greg replied grumpily.

"Come on, Greg. I think you could really make the team. You look strong for your size, and you move good. How much do you weigh?"

"Tim, knock it off, man. I haven't wrestled since sixth grade," Greg said, sliding his trash into the barrel, putting the silverware in the basin and the tray on the counter. "Besides, who wants to wrestle on those nasty mats anyway? Back home a couple of kids got a staph infection from wrestling. And I don't want to wear those stupid uniforms either."

"It ain't that bad, man. Those uniforms make you look muscular! Chicks dig men in tights!" Tim chuckled, following Greg with his tray.

"Besides, those excuses sound lame, Greg." Tim locked eyes with him in the cafeteria doorway. "Are you going to let Steve get to you?"

Greg didn't have an answer to that, because it was exactly the reason Greg wanted to stay as far away from wrestling as he could.

Tim gave him a steady look. "Steve thinks he's big stuff. I mean, he is a good wrestler. He came in third in regionals last year," Tim admitted with a shrug. "But if you can wrestle Steve, he'll leave you alone. It's win-win. You won't be some nerdy push-over, you can shut Steve up, and I bet Debbie will be pretty impressed, too."

* * * * *

As discussions on <u>The Outsiders</u> continued that week, Greg was pleased that Mrs. Harvan had put him and Debbie in the same group for the final project. On Wednesday their group started cutting pictures from magazines to illustrate themes from the book. Debbie and the other girl were organizing the pictures and dividing the poster board into quadrants for their collage. As they pushed the brightly-colored pictures around on the design, Greg watched everyone's hands as they reached in: his own dark brown ones, Debbie's pale olive-colored, Maria's almost as brown as his own, Chuck's pink and freckled. Once the Elmer's glue was in, all those colors looked really good together. No outsiders or insiders in the finished collage. Just a nice rich mix.

By lunchtime Friday, Greg had actually stirred up the courage for open mats. After school he changed into his sweatsuit and ambled into the cafeteria, staying on the edges of the group, trying to look casual among the thirty or so boys who were standing around talking and joking. With the mats already laid out and taped to the floor, Mr. Visconsi—no, here he must be *Coach* Visconsi—was setting up a scale near the back wall. Some of the guys took the cue and started to take off their shoes.

"Oh, man," Greg stewed. "I gave away my old wrestling shoes. I'm sunk."

Coach Visconsi's voice boomed over the chatter. "Boys, I need you to strip down to your underwear and weigh in. Then we'll pair you off and you'll wrestle a man the same size."

Greg's stomach went cold. He wished he hadn't come. The other guys clearly knew the drill, stripping down and getting in line by size. Greg didn't know how much he weighed, but an eyeball scan told him he might be a little heavier than average. He swallowed hard, and stepped in front of a hefty kid he knew from math, Kenny Stechlin, who had a mild face and seemed as gentle as a Saint Bernard.

"First weigh-in in a while?" asked Kenny.

"Haven't wrestled in a couple of years," Greg shrugged, trying to sound confident.

"It isn't that bad. It gets better. Soon you'll be used to locker rooms with naked guys," Kenny joked as the line snaked toward the scale.

Soon it was Greg's turn. As his dark brown feet stepped on the cold black scale, he shivered, taking deep breaths.

"One thirty-four!" yelled Coach Visconsi. "Son, you're a tweener! You could be useful."

Greg didn't know what a tweener was but he nodded and mumbled, "Thank you, sir."

Putting his t-shirt and sweatpants back on, Greg remembered the wrestling shoes.

"Hey, Kenny. How much did you weigh?" he asked, an empty question to give himself some traction.

"One fifty-six. Man, that's bigger than I thought." Kenny shook his head. "I don't want to hit heavyweight yet."

Bewildered—Greg had always thought the heavyweights pretty impressive guys—he still had his opening. "Do you have an extra pair of wrestling shoes? I, uh, forgot mine."

"Yeah, sure thing. These're nines," Kenny muttered, rifling through his gym bag. "They're from last year. Is that okay?"

"Thanks, man," Greg smiled, taking the soft shoes in hand, and lacing them on.

The coaches were huddled over a notebook at a cafeteria table, setting up a two-column chart for the wrestle-off. As soon as it was taped to the tile wall, all the wrestlers gathered to scan the pairings.

Immediately Steve Martucci's voice rang out. "Greg Young is wrestling me? Are you kidding? This is a joke, right? Does that kid even wrestle here?"

"Actually, he does," Tim Cassidy replied evenly.

"Since when does he wrestle? All he does is hang out with band geeks playing that stupid horn," Steve sneered, "and reading stupid books."

"Hey, Martucci, leave him alone." It was Kenny facing off with Steve. "Suck it up, man. Unless you're afraid he might beat you."

The challenge hung in the air.

Tim, and now Kenny: two friends Greg could count on.

Coach Visconsi stepped in. "Stechlin's right, Martucci. You're wrestling Young at 138 pounds. You know that's how we do it. If you don't want to wrestle Young, you can give him your starting spot."

Another challenge hung in the air.

After a long moment, Steve muttered, "Fine, I'll wrestle him."

The coaches started the wrestle-off by calling the two at 98 pounds. Greg sat as close as he could, watching the boys' moves, trying to remember moves and positions he had known two years ago. He found himself leaning left, then right, as the wrestlers jockeyed for position, aching and straining with the guy on the bottom, cheering silently as he escaped and pressed the other guy to the mat.

Too soon for Greg's taste, Coach called for the 138-pound match. "Okay, boys. Get on the mat and square off."

Kenny's shoes felt loose on Greg's feet, but they stuck to the mat and that's what mattered. Greg stood opposite Steve, shifting his weight from foot to foot, his hands loose, his mouth dry.

"Ready, set, *wrestle!*" Coach Visconsi blew his whistle to start the match.

Steve didn't charge the way Greg thought he would, instead balancing back and forth, facing Greg menacingly.

"Shoot on me. I dare you, black boy," mumbled Steve. Dancing lightly, Greg said nothing. "Come on, I know you can. I know you can shoot on me." Greg stayed quiet, his eyes locked on Steve's. Then Steve dove in, butting Greg's face with the heel of his hand and going for Greg's lead leg, his left.

Suddenly Greg was off balance, struggling to stay upright. Steve was lifting Greg's leg higher and higher, so that Greg had to turn with his face full away. And that's when Steve went for the takedown, sweeping Greg's leg out from under him, dropping him hard on his stomach. Steve held him flat.

"Got ya now, black boy," Steve growled, reaching under Greg's belly.

Suddenly Greg was aware of the other guys yelling all around him. He picked out Kenny's bellow: "Grab his hands!" Reaching back and under, Greg seized both of Steve's wrists. And he heard Tim: "Reach back and roll right!" Much to Greg's amazement, he pulled off a fat man roll and abruptly found himself on top, and for an instant, Steve's back was flat on the mat.

The rest of the boys in the cafeteria were going crazy, hollering and slapping the floor. Greg realized he was actually winning. His throat felt tight as he strengthened his grip on Steve's wrists. But immediately Steve surged, flipped Greg and flattened him. Coach Visconsi's face was inches from his own, his eyes locked on Greg's shoulder blades as Greg arched his back, straining against Steve's pressure. Flat on his belly, Coach was counting with the flat of his hand against the mat. Then he raised his right arm, calling the pin.

Steve leaped to his feet. From the corner of his eye, Greg saw Steve's little victory dance off to the edge of the mat. He couldn't hear what Steve was saying, which was just as well. Greg pulled himself up, his eyes glued to the floor. Maybe wrestling wasn't what he wanted to do this fall any way.

Coach Visconsi bellowed, "Next match, 145 pounds!"

Greg went looking for the chair where he'd left his sweatsuit, breathing hard but quiet inside. "Those guys had my back against Steve. I did all right." But still, losing hurt.

* * * * *

The weekend came and went, but Greg's dad stayed in Columbus for an additional sales conference, so there was no family outing. Monday morning came, and after Mrs. Young dropped Keith and Judy at Lowden, Greg was quiet in the car. He didn't like the silence, and he could see his mother's anxiety, but he didn't trust his voice or his heart. Homeroom came and went, and math, and English, and band. There was an English test on vocabulary and compound-complex sentences, so he didn't have to talk to Debbie. Miss Burgess was annoyed with the whole wind section and kept them halfway through lunch, so he didn't have to talk to Tim, either. Then the afternoon came and went, and Greg could taste dismissal.

The bell was still echoing as Greg dodged through the mayhem of the corridors, desperate to get to the parking lot, to the safety of his mom's station wagon. Still stung by Friday's wrestling debacle, Greg kept his eyes on the terrazzo floor, his book bag slung over his shoulder. He could see the glass doors just beyond the main office. He was nearly safe.

But then he recognized Steve Martucci silhouetted in the doorway, talking to Debbie.

Greg froze.

"Hey, Greg!" Steve's voice. *He wants to rub it in.* Greg cringed.

"Leave him alone, Steve!" Debbie hissed. "Just leave him alone."

"I want to talk to the guy. Anything wrong with that?" Steve retorted.

Greg continued toward the door, and all three stepped into the chilly gray afternoon. "Yeah?" Greg said, trying to keep his voice emotionless.

Steve took a few steps toward the asphalt, his hands in his pockets, and turned back. It wasn't exactly a swagger, but Greg braced for the taunt lurking behind Steve's half-grin.

98

Steve looked Greg up and down, silently. "Good match Friday. I didn't know you had it in you, man. Shake?" And he stretched out his hand.

Greg caught a glimpse of Debbie's fluorescent blue eyes over Steve's shoulder. She was smiling. Greg's own charcoaled eyes eased into a smile, and for the first time he almost felt content in this dungeon they called school. He reached out his hand.

"Thanks, man. Thanks for taking me on."

Appendix

Suggested Exercises to Accompany "An Invitation and A Decision: A Story of South Euclid in 1883"

from *Grade 7 Concepts __Ohio Learning Standards: Science__*
The movement of water through the spheres of Earth is known as the hydrologic cycle... Ground water and surface water quality are important components of the hydrologic cycle. The porosity and permeability of the rock and/or soil (grade 6) can affect the rate at which the water flows... Relating water flow to geographic and topographic landforms and/or features leads to an understanding of where water flows and how it moves through the different spheres. Topographic and aerial maps (can be virtual) can be used to identify drainage patterns and watersheds that contribute to the cycling of water.

Build a model to represent a cross-section of Earth's surface (soil, rock, surface, ground water) that can enable investigation of multiple water pathways. Explain and demonstrate to the class.

Study the attached photos, diagrams, and map. Then work together to build a model of the Welch Woods segment of the Euclid Creek Metropark. Use different colors to show the different layers of rock in the cliff wall.

Profile Section across the Cuyahoga Valley.

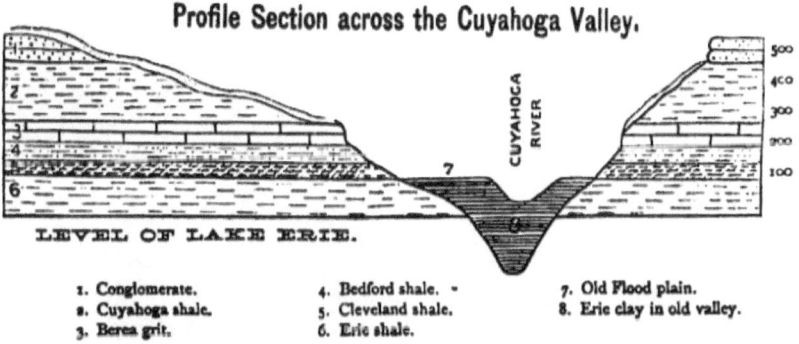

1. Conglomerate.
2. Cuyahoga shale.
3. Berea grit.
4. Bedford shale.
5. Cleveland shale.
6. Erie shale.
7. Old Flood plain.
8. Erie clay in old valley.

Diagram from the Report of the Geological Survey of Ohio 1873. Vol 1. p. 172.

BEDFORD SHALE IN OLD QUARRY ON EUCLID CREEK, 1¼ MILES NORTH OF SOUTH EUCLID

View looking southeast. About 12 feet of the "Euclid bluestone" shows above the water level, one massive layer, overlain by thinner layers with shale partings; above lies 20 feet of soft blue shale, with here and there thin bands of flags or concretions. Above the uppermost of these bands the shale is red, soft, and homogeneous and passes upward into the thin sheet of overlying boulder clay.

Photo from Geology and Mineral Resources of the Cleveland District, Ohio, by H.P. Cushing, Frank Leverett, and Frank R. Van Horn (U.S. Geological Survey, Bulletin 818, 1931), plate 3 (between pages 40-41).

Devonian-age Chagrin shale forms most of the valley wall in Euclid Creek Reservation in Euclid.
The Bedford and Berea formations form the upper part of this gorge.

Photo from <u>Roadside Geology of Ohio,</u> by Mark J. Camp (Mountain Press Publishing Co., 2006), p. 321.

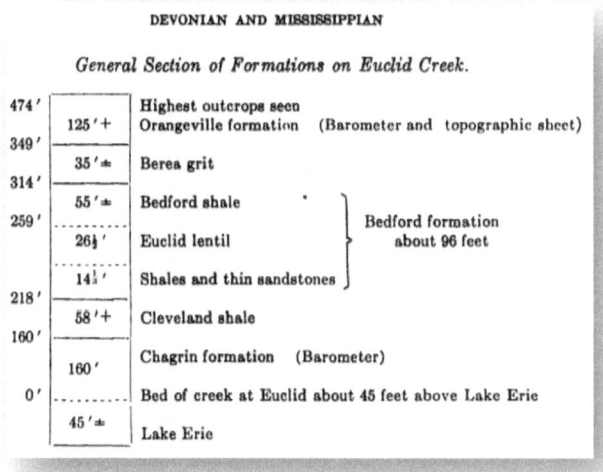

DEVONIAN AND MISSISSIPPIAN

General Section of Formations on Euclid Creek.

474'		Highest outcrops seen
	125'+	Orangeville formation (Barometer and topographic sheet)
349'		
	35'±	Berea grit
314'		
	55'±	Bedford shale
259'		} Bedford formation
	26½'	Euclid lentil } about 96 feet
	14½'	Shales and thin sandstones }
218'		
	58'+	Cleveland shale
160'		
	160'	Chagrin formation (Barometer)
0'		Bed of creek at Euclid about 45 feet above Lake Erie
	45'±	Lake Erie

Chart from the <u>Report of the Geological Survey of Ohio</u> 1873. Vol 1.

Suggested Exercises to Accompany "It Was Worth It: A Story of South Euclid in 1915"

*Mathematics. Statistics and Probability 7. **Ohio Learning Standards***
3. *Informally assess the degree of visual overlap of two numerical data distributions with similar variabilities, measuring the difference between the centers by expressing it as a multiple of a measure of variability.*
4. *Use measures of center and measures of variability for numerical data from random samples to draw informal comparative inferences about two populations.*

   A. Compare the American League standings from 1914 and 1915. In 1914 Nap Lajoie played for Cleveland, and in 1915 he played for Philadelphia. What conclusion could you draw about his impact on each team's success?

American League Standings 1914				
Team	**Wins**	**Losses**	**%**	**Games behind**
Philadelphia Athletics	99	53	.651	--
Boston Red Sox	91	62	.595	8.5
Washington Senators	81	73	.526	19.0
Detroit Tigers	80	73	.523	19.5
St. Louis Browns	71	82	.464	28.5
New York Yankees	70	84	.455	30.0
Chicago White Sox	70	84	.455	30.0
Cleveland Naps	51	102	.333	48.5

American League Standings 1915

Team	Wins	Losses	%	Games behind
Boston Red Sox	101	50	.669	--
Detroit Tigers	100	54	.659	2.5
Chicago White Sox	93	61	.604	9.5
Washington Senators	85	68	.556	17.0
New York Yankees	69	83	.454	32.5
St. Louis Browns	63	91	.409	39.5
Cleveland Indians	57	95	.375	44.5
Philadelphia Athletics	43	109	.283	58.5

http://www.baseball-reference.com/leagues/AL

Social Studies. Spatial Thinking and Skills Gr. 7 <u>*Ohio Learning Standards*</u>

12. *Maps and other geographic representations can be used to trace the development of human settlement over time.*

   A. Look at a map of the United States and locate the American League cities in 1914-1915. What geographic pattern do you see? What explanation can you give for the limits on the locations of major league teams?

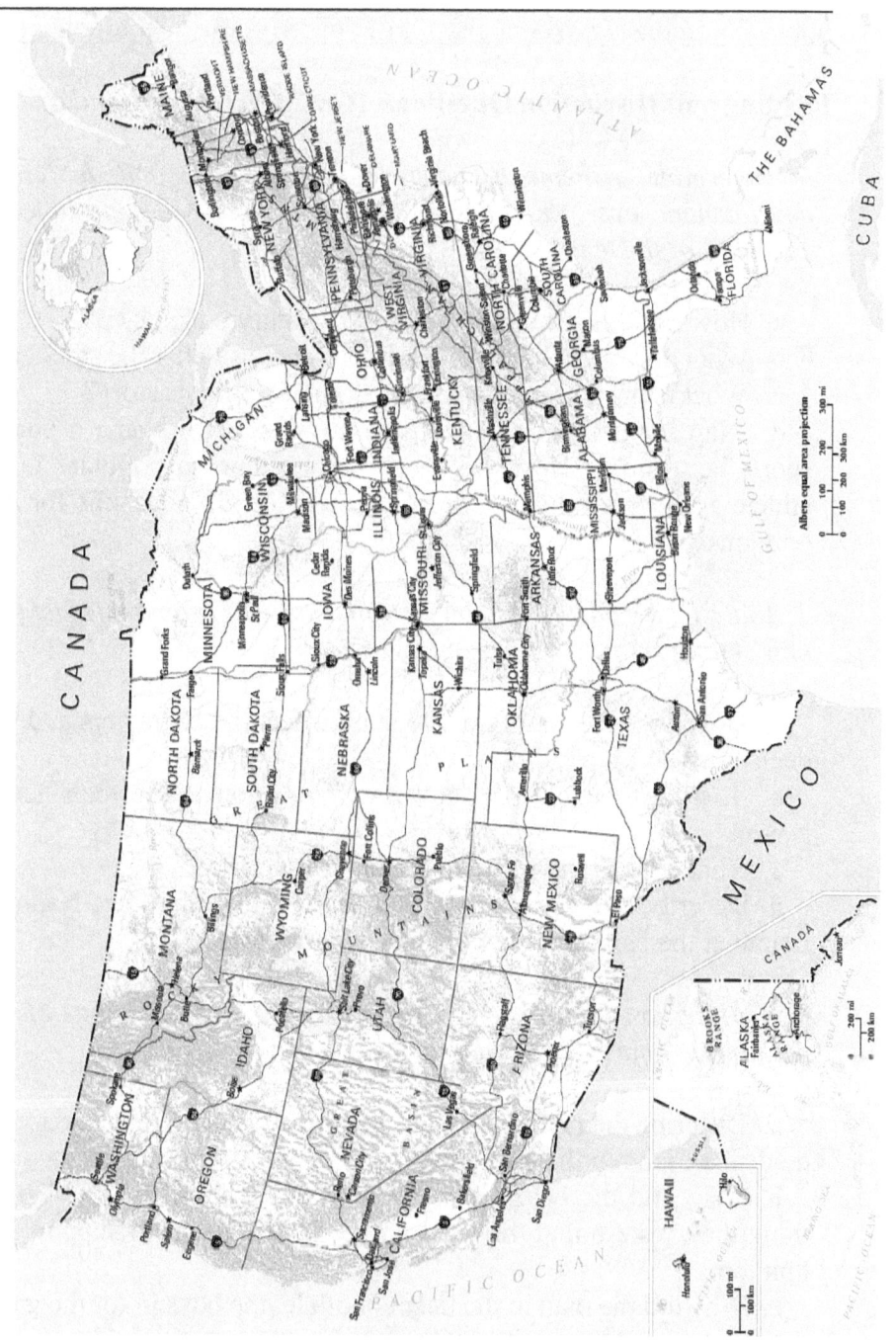

Reading and Discussion Questions (*Gr. 7 Literature Standards*)

2. Determine a theme or central idea of a text and analyze its development over the course of the text; provide an objective summary of the text.

   a. How does the title give a clue to the story's theme?
   b. What do you predict will happen to the boys after the story ends?
   c. What is the lesson that can be learned from this story?
   d. Nap Lajoie was a hero to the boys in 1915. Name a popular sports hero today. How did he or she become so popular? Is this athlete a good role model for young people? Give reasons for your opinions.

3. Analyze how particular elements of a story or drama interact (e.g., how setting shapes the characters or plot).

   a. How does the setting of the story affect the characters and their decisions?
   b. List the struggles the boys faced in order to see their hero in person.
   c. What does Frankie add to the plot of the story?
   d. Describe the emotions the boys felt when they met Napoleon Lajoie at the ballpark. Find evidence in the text.

6. Analyze how an author develops and contrasts the points of view of different characters or narrators in a text.

   a. Describe the personalities of the three main characters based on evidence found in the text.
   b. Why did the boys lie to the man in the ticket booth? Do you think they were doing the right thing? Give reasons to support your opinion.
   c. Why did the man in the ticket booth let the boys in for the game? Was he being irresponsible? Give reasons to support your opinion.

Suggested Exercises to Accompany "Finding the Courage: A Story of South Euclid in 1925"

STATISTICS AND PROBABILITY 7.SP: <u>*Ohio Learning*</u>
<u>*Standards: Mathematics*</u>
Use random sampling to draw inferences about a population.
   1. Understand that statistics can be used to gain information about a population by examining a sample of the population; generalizations about a population from a sample are valid only if the sample is representative of that population. Understand that random sampling tends to produce representative samples and support valid inferences.

   Study the following chart describing the population of Cleveland in the early twentieth century.*

year	Cleveland's total population	Cleveland's foreign-born population *
1890	261,353	97,095
1910	560,663	196,170
1920	796,841	

   A. In 1890, what proportion of Cleveland's population was born outside the U.S.?

   B. In 1910, what proportion of Cleveland's population was born outside the U.S.?

   C. Assuming a similar rate of change between 1890 and 1910, what would you expect the foreign-born population of Cleveland to be in 1920?

*Edward M. Miggins and Mary Morgenthaler. "The Ethnic Mosaic: The Settlement of Cleveland by the New Immigrants and Migrants." 105. In **Thomas F. Campbell and Edward M. Miggins. The Birth of Modern Cleveland 1865-1930**. Cleveland: WRHS, 1988.*

D. For its 1921 Year Book, the Cleveland Foundation used data from a 1915 police census and other local sources to estimate the 1920 population of the city. (Data from the 1920 Federal Census was not yet available.) Study this table.

Major Ethnic Groups in Cleveland's Population (rounded numbers, estimated in 1920 from 1915 local census data)

The Cleveland Year Book 1921. The Cleveland Foundation, 1921.

Total estimated population	640,300	100%
German	150,000	
English/Irish/Scottish	100,000	
Polish	65,000	
Bohemian	60,000	
Jewish	46,000	
Hungarian	45,000	
Slovak	35,000	
African-American	34,000	
Slovenian	30,000	
Italian	24,000	
Lithuanian	12,000	
Croatian	10,000	
Russian	10,000	
Ukrainian	10,000	
Romanian	9,000	
Asian	300	
Other	28,000	

What percentage of the total is each ethnic group?

E. Imagine that you had a school of 500 children in which the ethnic population of the student body matched the ethnic distribution of the city as a whole. How many children of each ethnic background would make up the student body of 500 children?

Total enrollment	500	100%
German		
English/Irish/Scottish		
Polish		
Bohemian		
Jewish		
Hungarian		
Slovak		
African-American		
Slovenian		
Italian		
Lithuanian		
Croatian		
Russian		
Ukrainian		
Romanian		
Asian		
Other		

In 1920 the actual foreign born population was 256,531.

Suggested Exercises to Accompany "Farewells and New Beginnings: A Story of South Euclid in 1949"

Historical Thinking and Skills Grade 7 <u>*Ohio Learning Standards: Social Studies*</u>
Content Statement:
1. Historians and archaeologists describe historical events and issues from the perspectives of people living at the time to avoid evaluating the past in terms of today's norms and values.

Spatial Thinking and Skills Grade 7 <u>*Ohio Learning Standards: Social Studies*</u>
Content Statement:
12. Maps and other geographic representations can be used to trace the development of human settlement over time.

Civic Participation and Skills Grade 7 <u>*Ohio Learning Standards: Social Studies*</u>
Content Statement:
16. The ability to understand individual and group perspectives is essential to analyzing historic and contemporary issues.

When immigrants came to Cleveland, a number of factors influenced where they rented a room, an apartment or a house. They had to be near a main street so they could reach the streetcars to get to work. They wanted to live near other people who spoke the same language, and probably came from the same town or region in the old country. And many people wanted a place of worship—church or synagogue—where the prayers were in the language they spoke. Observant Orthodox Jews needed to be within walking distance of a synagogue.

In "Farewells and New Beginnings" Joe Stein's family has moved from Glenville to Holmden Road in South Euclid, where they would become members of the Warrensville Center Synagogue. That congregation would eventually include members of eight different immigrant congregations from the Glenville and Mt. Pleasant neighborhoods of Cleveland.

Study this map of Mt. Pleasant. Locate each of the following synagogue sites, using colored pencils or markers as indicated.

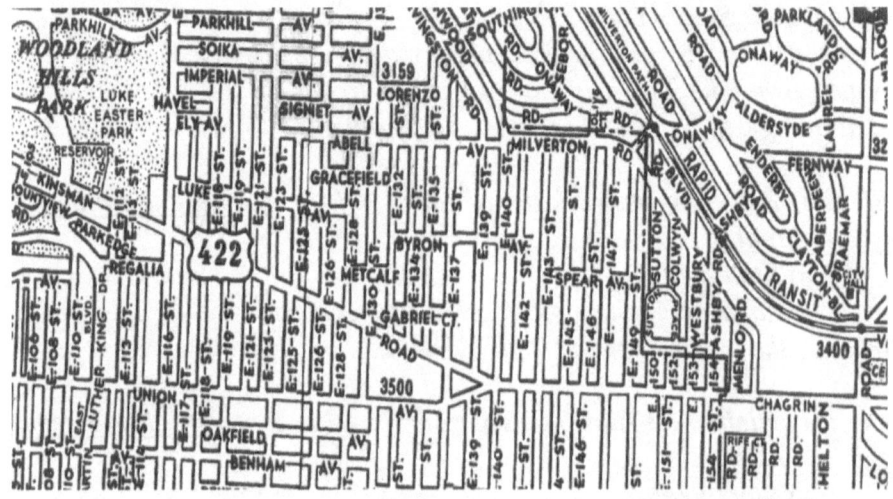

A. Lithuanian immigrants started a synagogue on E. 118 between Kinsman and Union in 1922. **(green)**
B. Hungarian immigrants started a synagogue at E. 149 and Kinsman in 1930. **(green)**
C. Russian immigrants moved their synagogue to E. 140 and Kinsman in 1925. **(red)**
D. Polish immigrants started a synagogue at. E. 119 and Union in 1920. **(red)**
E. Russian immigrants started a synagogue at E. 149 and Kinsman in 1919. **(yellow)**
F. Russian immigrants built a synagogue at E. 118 and Kinsman in 1923. **(yellow)** They moved to a new building at E. 135 and Kinsman in 1932. **(yellow)**

Notice how close to one another these synagogues were.

In 1930 the members of each synagogue were probably immigrants from Lithuania, Poland, Russia and Hungary who were not fluent in speaking or understanding English. Their sons and daughters would be attending Cleveland public schools in 1930.

Imagine that the average member of each synagogue was 40 years old in 1930.
→ How old would these men be in 1950?

Imagine that a member of one congregation in 1930 had children who were 12 and 9 years old.
→ How old would the children be in 1950?

Question:
By 1950, what has changed in the membership of these synagogues that would allow Russian and Polish and Lithuanian and Hungarian Jews to form one congregation for worship?

References

The writers used a wide variety of sources in researching their stories—print, electronic, human, and brick-and-mortar—but the following sources were useful to the authors of all of the stories in this collection.

Encyclopedia of Cleveland History. http://ech.cwru.edu/

Larick, Roy, with Bob Gibbons and Edward Siplock. Euclid Creek. Images of America. Arcadia, 2005.

The Proud Heritage of South Euclid, Ohio. City of South Euclid, [1967].

Schuemann, Nancy L. On the Threshold of a New Century: The City of South Euclid 1967-1999. August Graphics, 1999.

South Euclid-Lyndhurst Historical Society. South Euclid. Images of America. Arcadia, 2011.

www.ingramcontent.com/pod-product-compliance
Lightning Source LLC
Chambersburg PA
CBHW031835170626
46807CB00004B/1465